THE COTTAGE OF SECRETS

THE COTTAGE OF SECRETS

MARIAN COLLIHOLE

Matador
9 Priory Business Park,
Wistow Road, Kibworth Beauchamp,
Leicestershire. LE8 0RX
Tel: (+44) 116 279 2299
Fax: (+44) 116 279 2277
Email: books@troubador.co.uk
Web: www.troubador.co.uk/matador

ISBN 9781785891786

British Library Cataloguing in Publication Data.
A catalogue record for this book is available from the British Library.

Cover illustration by Dave Hill
www.davehillsart.co.uk

Typeset in 11pt Aldine by Troubador Publishing Ltd, Leicester, UK
Printed and bound by CPI Group (UK) Ltd, Croydon, CR0 4YY

Matador is an imprint of Troubador Publishing Ltd

For Anne

CONTENTS

THE COTTAGE OF SECRETS

The old man and woman sat in opposite corners of the inglenook, but their companionship was one of a strange blankness. Despite the warmth of the glowing coal fire, they sat as though dead, seemingly without thought or emotion. Nor did they display any interest in the domestic activities of Lottie, their young housekeeper, as she bustled around them in the cottage's sunless room.

She was tugging now at the heavy velvet curtains, trying to draw them further apart. She thought how much brighter the room could be if she could let in the flashes of yellow sunshine, darting here and there through the fluttering shadows of the trees outside. She tugged again, but the curtains were too wide. She turned to complain to the old couple, but with a resigned shrug, she changed her mind and disappeared into the kitchen to prepare tea.

From the kitchen window she could see nothing but a high brick wall, which effectively blocked out any sun from that side of the house. The kitchen was chilled, even in summer, chilled and cheerless, she thought as she sliced a loaf with exasperated speed.

When her husband Bert came in, she would tell him again, only this time she would be definite. Old people or no, she would not stay in this house much longer. If leaving the cottage meant Bert having to lose his job in the small holding, well what would that matter compared with the endless, dreary days spent in this dark, decaying place. The way the old people sat staring into worlds of their own most of the time could be scary. Then they would suddenly rouse themselves whenever she was about to do something which would not meet with their approval.

Thinking about it now, she realised that for the first time, neither of them had reacted when she was trying to let in more sunshine. Usually, they would both start shaking their heads vehemently and the old man would shriek out in that querulous, quivering voice of his, that their eyes were too weak to face the sun. Today they had just continued to sit in silence, their bloodless lips unmoving in parchment masks, completely withdrawn.

"How strange!" she mused. Perhaps they were getting used to having her about the house.

Her reverie was broken by the demanding tapping of a stick against the chimney in the nook.

"It is nearly ready," she called out. "I'll be there in half a tic." Hurriedly, she covered the thin slices of bread with the strange mushroom paste that was the couple's staple diet. Apart from fruit from the garden and a seed cake made from an ancient recipe, and despite having a smallholding full of vegetables, they ate nothing else.

Luckily, Bert made enough for their wages by selling the produce to the local shops nearby.

Methodically, she now made the tea and carried the tray into the living room. She set it down on a small table at the old man's elbow. He was leaning forward to tear off yesterday's calendar page.

Again, she wondered idly about the couple's strange habits.

"Why," she asked herself, "did he always wait until this hour to correct the date?" She knew it was deliberate, for he seemed obsessed with the calendar, forever watching it through his small eyes.

Lottie knew better than to pause to enquire. His response would be that eerie glare, which she confessed to herself, she found unnerving. She was always glad to return to the kitchen, despite its lack of cheerful light. Bert would be home soon and so she began to prepare his meal. Besides, she knew that the old ones liked to eat in peace and quiet.

"Old ones?" she thought suddenly. "I don't think I have ever seen the old lady eat a thing. How much of the tea would the old lady eat?" she wondered. "Her lips look too dry to allow food to pass them." She broke off her reflection and set about peeling potatoes.

In the darkening, middle room, the old man picked up the sandwiches. Slowly, he ate his way through them, taking one from each plate in turn. Then, he poured out the tea into two cups, before sipping from each of the cups in turn. Throughout, the old lady sat unmoving, her rheumy eyes vacant and staring into space.

The clock chimed five o'clock. Already, the evenings were drawing in and their faces were barely discernible in the gloom. They sat in silence for a while until Lottie came and took away the tray.

Then the old man spoke, his voice dry and crackly with age. Still, it penetrated the stillness of the room, like an icy shard of glass.

"Barely six hours to go now, my beloved." The words were at odds with the raucous monotone and the thread of menace that seemed to underlie it. Slowly then, he raised himself up out of the chair and struggled towards the window on his weak legs.

The burly figure of Bert was striding up the path and he waved to the old man, before entering the kitchen. Like Lottie, he too was becoming aware of both a sense of foreboding that hung about the cottage and also the increasingly odd behaviour of the couple. Over the last few days, he had felt nervous in a way he had not known before and he knew Lottie was also uneasy. Yet he would describe neither of them as fanciful. Being almost spooked was alien to them both.

He could not help feeling guilty that Lottie had been willing to come to this isolated cottage for his sake. He had hoped to gain enough experience to start up his own smallholding. Lottie had cheerfully accepted the old couple's strange withdrawn behaviour and relied on keeping herself busy until he came back in the early evenings.

Now he realised that they had been there for almost a month and that during the last few days, a subtle change had crept over the couple. Sometimes, he thought he detected a glint of evil in the old man's eyes, and a weird feeling of an almost electrically charged atmosphere in the cottage. It was rather like the eerie quietness before a thunderstorm. Yet this was in contrast to the pleasant autumn evenings.

Priding himself on being a stable, realistic man, he found that something was now urging him to get away. He put his head around the doorway and called a friendly greeting to the couple. As usual, the old woman sat immobile, but her husband turned his head towards Bert and acknowledged him with a thin smile. His eyes smiled too and Bert found himself staring into the gloom, yet still able to see a malevolent gleam in the oldster's yellowing eyes. For a moment, his gaze was held hypnotically. Then, abruptly, he turned back into the kitchen. His mind was made up. They would go to his mother's house and what's more, they would go tonight.

He whispered his decision to Lottie and was rewarded by seeing her face light up. They picked at their food as they made their plans.

Inside the living room, the old man heard the whispering and smiled. He was glad on two counts. There was no need for the young people to make plans, and he had made his own plans as late as the day before yesterday. Why he had not thought of it before, he could not imagine, but he thought he had solved what had been an enormous problem for almost a hundred years.

Now, he hobbled into the kitchen, startling the young couple, neither of whom could hide their sudden fear. However he shuffled past them with a nod and disappeared into the old pantry which was never used. It was kept locked and Lottie had glimpsed inside it only once before. All she had seen was a wall covered in cobwebs and insects scurrying across the floor. Then the door had been firmly closed, blocking her view.

When the old man re-emerged, he was carrying an old jar, half hidden inside his coat. Nodding to them again, he smiled at them and for the first time, Lottie and Bert thought the smile seemed almost genuine, but it was too fleeting for them to be sure. They continued with their plans and by nine o'clock they were ready to leave.

They had debated long and hard as to whether they should tell the old people that they were leaving and would arrange for someone to replace them as soon as they could. They had argued to themselves that the old couple were too weak to hurt them and eventually decided to say farewell in person.

The clock was actually chiming nine o'clock, when they tapped on the living room door and went hesitantly into the darkened room. The lamps had not been lit and they could neither see nor hear anything.

Tentatively, they crept in, thinking the couple must be fast asleep. Then they heard a sigh and a gasp. Looking at each other, they hurriedly lit the two lamps either side of the room. Realisation came to them both at the same time. The fire was dying out, but the couple were past that. They were not asleep. They had died together and in their death, they were both smiling, the first real smiles that Bert and Lottie had seen from them.

"Are they really dead?" asked Lottie, afraid to touch them in case it was some kind of trick, but Bert nodded.

"Yes, Lottie and they look at peace."

"I don't understand," cried Lottie. "They were both alright at teatime. What could have happened? This is so weird."

Lottie hung behind Bert as if she expected the couple to suddenly jump up at them, but Bert was looking at the floor. A glass jar had rolled down between the old folks in the inglenook. He picked it up using his handkerchief in case the receding heat from the fire was still hot enough to burst the glass, but although it was warm it was intact.

"What are those inside it?" asked Lottie, peering over his shoulder. "Ugh, they look like dead cockroaches!"

"Weirder and weirder," replied Bert slowly, as if trying to understand exactly what could have happened. "What was he doing with cockroaches? He must have found them in the old pantry but why? It is all a mystery to me. We must call for an ambulance and I think the police as well."

Whilst they were waiting, Bert tried to arrange the couple so that they appeared sitting up. It was then that he noticed an old envelope sticking out of the old man's pocket. It was addressed to him and Lottie in quivery handwriting and dated only the day before yesterday. Inside was a newspaper cutting dated a hundred years before and scrawled across the top was a handwritten message.

"This will explain all. Excerpt from the Saturday Observer."

To their utter astonishment, the article was dated exactly one hundred years before. They took it into the kitchen, taking the lamps with them and sat down together to read.

"Today, at exactly 9 p.m. the Black Arts Society announced a curse should be put on Alfred and Winnie Browning. The elderly, and almost infirm couple, would live for a further hundred years exactly as they were today. The Black Arts Society informed its members that Alfred and Winnie had caused the death of their leader by wrongly using a curse on him in temper. As retribution, they would live for a hundred years and a further hundred after that unless the curse was lifted by them killing again on the day they were due to die."

Even before they looked at the heading again, Bert and Lottie knew that the date was exactly hundred years before to the hour the Black Arts Leader had died. They re-read the clipping three or four times trying to make sense of it.

Slowly, a realisation dawned on them. The old man had been planning to kill one or both of them until he too had re-read the curse put on him. Sometime during the last few days, he had noticed that the curse did not specify that a human being had to be killed. He had risked the possibility of having to endure another hundred years of living in the gloom and despair of infirmity, by interpreting the demand to the letter.

Yes, he had killed. Yes it was a hundred years later. Yes it happened at exactly nine o'clock. But he had chosen to kill two cockroaches.

"Thank you, old man," whispered Bert. "You spared our lives. Rest in Peace."

REVENGE

PART ONE

Judy took the blows silently. She was past even the smallest whimper or groan. Indeed, she scarcely felt pain or fear. She was impervious to the swelling discomfort of her right eye, to the broken skin on her badly bruised cheeks. She could not even feel relief that this time, he had missed her ribs, for some reason concentrating his blows on to her face, her neck and her shoulders. She felt nothing because she made herself feel nothing.

Later, when she was sure he had left the house, she struggled to her feet. As she stood unsteadily clutching the table, she acknowledged for the first time, the pain in her jaw, the stinging in her cheeks, the raw ache of broken skin and the shaking that suddenly attacked her whole body. She acknowledged but she did not suffer, for this was the last time he would hit her and soon, very soon, he would know it too.

She walked on rubbery legs into the kitchen and made herself a hot, sweet cup of tea. Then she sat down and let the comforting liquid bring back a little strength to her. The shuddering of her body ceased. This time, there was no echoing shudder of her mind either. The time for trembling was over, unless of course it was his. When she had finished her tea, she made no attempt to clean herself up. She would let him see what he had done when he returned from his lunchtime boozing. Instead, she called a taxi and made no attempt to hide her face from the embarrassed driver. The more people who saw her today, the better.

It took the driver a few minutes into the journey before he pulled back the protective window between passenger and front seat and asked if she was alright.

"Shouldn't I be taking you to the hospital, Miss?" He had seen too much of domestic violence to probe with other questions he knew would go unanswered.

Pain hit her now as she shook her head. Although he had barely touched her body, she ached all over and the pain in her face throbbed incessantly and unpleasantly. She felt a nausea sweep over her. The driver closed the window with a shrug and drove more quickly, but giving an occasional glance into his mirror as if to make sure she was alright.

Judy stopped the cab at the corner of a large supermarket. She paid the driver with a grateful smile, so that he would know that his sympathy had registered with her and watched him drive off. Then she turned the corner into a side road and jumped quickly into the waiting Mini.

"My God," whispered the woman driving, as she caught a glimpse of her friend's face. The car wobbled as the shock hit her, but Judy urged her on, slinking into her seat and hoping that no one had seen her get into the car.

An hour later, they were calmly going over their plans. Both were more determined than ever, that which had once seemed a harebrained idea should turn now into a definite commitment. Felicity had taken her friend's photograph, showing the fast colouring injuries from different angles. She had only seen her friend's face injured once before and that had just been a blackened, half closed eye. She had been appalled then. She was even more shocked now.

Felicity and Judy had been friends at school. Then Felicity had gone away to work in Leeds and the two had lost contact. She had been back in Halifax for two years but the two had never met until a month before, when she had come face to face with a battered woman she hardly recognised, who had tried to walk past, ashamed and not wanting to talk. But Felicity had insisted on taking her home to her flat. There she and her best friend Mel had listened to the story of a romance that had gone sour. Judy, it appeared, had been subjected to beatings almost from the first week she had moved in with Ron Andrews.

It was Mel who had asked why she did not leave him. The answer had been simple.

"I have no money of my own," Judy had replied. "Ron won't allow me to work. He is afraid I will make friends and become less dependent upon him. I have thought of leaving him, Mel, many times, I can assure you."

Felicity was not prepared to leave things as they were, but there was one question she had to ask first, so she had come straight to the point.

"You are not alone now, so the possibility becomes more positive." Mel, although she had only just met Judy for the first time, nodded in agreement as Felicity went on. "We hear of so many cases of battered women returning to their husbands or boyfriends after being found refuge, that we have to consider, would you ever go back to him?"

Judy had shuddered at the words 'battered women'. She felt ashamed and degraded that she had allowed herself to earn such a description. She found the word refuge equally distasteful. She did not want to leave the control of one person only to hand over her destiny to others.

"I would never return. I have no feelings for him other that loathing. Even so, leaving is such a giant step. Without your help, I would never consider it, but without being ungrateful, I need to take control of my own life. Otherwise, I may never gain my self-respect."

Felicity had understood her friend's feelings exactly. That is when the three of them had begun to work out a plan to deal with Ron and enable Judy to take charge of her own life. The sight of the new injuries today spurred them on. Hesitation and doubts were pushed aside. It was time to act.

"It must be tonight. Agreed?" asked Felicity, and when the other two nodded, she got out paper and pen and began making lists, following suggestions from Judy and Mel, so that Judy could really feel she was doing her own manoeuvring. They had talked it through every Wednesday since that first meeting. It was the only afternoon Felicity and Mel had off from the office. Writing and consultation and last minute alterations over, Felicity drove Judy to within a few minutes of her home. It was imperative that they were not seen together, or Ron would not get his comeuppance!

Judy did not immediately let herself into the house, although time was precious. There was one other thing she needed to do first. So she knocked on her neighbour's door and waited nervously on the step. The houses were three storey and she heard footsteps coming for quite a while before the door opened.

The middle-aged lady who opened the door gazed at Judy's face with open mouthed shock. They did not know each other well, but were friendly enough to exchange greetings when they did meet. Mrs. Matthews looked embarrassed as if not quite knowing what to say, but her concern was obvious.

"My poor child. Do come in," she offered, pushing the door open wider behind her. But Judy shook her head. Although it still hurt her to move her neck, she exaggerated the pain with a marked wince. She wanted Mrs. Matthews to remember her well.

"I'm sorry to bother you, Mrs. Matthews," she said in almost a whisper, "but I wanted to ask you not to mention to Ron that you've seen what he did to my face. I know you saw me last time and I'm so worried that you or your husband might say something to him, only you mustn't, not ever. He'll kill me if he thinks anyone else has seen me. He told me to stay in. Please, you won't say anything, will you?"

Mrs. Matthews had time only to shake her head obligingly, before Judy had fled into the house next door. She called out words of encouragement, but they were lost. The irony of Judy actually going out of her way to show her the injuries and then asking her not to say anything was lost to her, but the memory of bruising and scrages and hurt, remained with her.

Inside the house, Judy was busy. Gathering just a cross-section of clothes into a plastic bin bag, she moved from drawer to drawer. It was important that she only took a few clothes. She added one shoulder bag and just one or two new cosmetics she had been saving. Then she reached beneath the bed in the spare room and fished out a brand new suitcase already packed, mostly with clothes Ron had never seen. There were not many for she had refused to allow Felicity or Mel to lend her too much money, but there were enough with the other garments she had salvaged. Satisfied at last, she carried the bag and suitcase down the back garden, placing them just inside the back gate. Checking that she wasn't being overlooked, and hoping Mrs. Matthews was on the phone reporting to her husband what she had seen, she opened the back gate and left the items in the lane. No sooner had she gone racing back up the garden and into the house, than Mel had drawn up in her car and had placed the bag and suitcase in the boot. Then Mel drove about a mile away and sat in the car reading a magazine.

Judy checked that the casserole was in the oven. But first, she had sprinkled the casserole with a liberal helping of liver salts and then she turned up the oven higher than usual. She needed Ron to be able to smell his evening meal cooking when he got back from his job as afternoon barman at the Club. She did not relish another beating, though usually he showed some remorse after a heavy beating and left her alone for a while. She made sure her coat was hanging on the kitchen door. Ron always went straight upstairs to shower. He was very unlikely to go into the kitchen. She kept her fingers crossed that he would follow his normal pattern, otherwise their plan would have little chance of working.

It was not long before he came into the house, yelling her name. To his credit, he did stop short when she came into the hall to meet him but there was no apology. She did not meet his stare for fear of annoying him. Instead she told him his meal was almost ready, and she was just about to lay the table.

He allowed himself a grunted, "Good," then hurried upstairs. In truth, her injuries had both shocked and excited him. He felt powerful. Remorse flitted in and then out almost as quickly. He hadn't meant to hit her, but he knew it gave him pleasure and that he would do it again.

He emptied his pockets, leaving the notes and loose change on the dressing table. Then he left his clothes on the bed. Let Judy see to them. It would give her something to do.

As soon as he let himself into the bathroom and

she heard the shower hissing, Judy ran up the stairs as quietly as she could. Her movements were decisive. First she opened his wardrobe and removed the large tin box inside. Then she scooped up his discarded work clothes and dropped them onto the floor, once she had located the wallet in his back pocket. Then she fled down the stairs. In a few moments, she was out through the garden gate, into the returning Mel's car and they were away.

PART TWO

F elicity let two days pass before she went to the police station. She introduced herself to the Desk Sergeant and when she had briefly explained the reason for her visit, eventually found herself being interviewed in a small room, bare apart from a table and four chairs and a lamp swinging low from the ceiling. The room was barred and there were no curtains, but she didn't find it intimidating. Her story was well rehearsed but even so, she was afraid she might lose concentration if she allowed other thoughts to keep in. She ignored her surroundings and fixed her eyes on the policeman and policewoman seated opposite her. Unlike in the films she had seen on television there was no further officer standing guard by the door.

"You've no objection to the interview being recorded, have you, Miss Howells?" was the detective's opening query, and when she had shaken her head with a small smile, he switched it on.

"I think it will save time if you will tell us your concerns uninterrupted and then we can question you further, later on," he spoke decisively. "I am Sergeant Jones and this is Police Constable Collier, soon to be promoted herself. Speak clearly and not too fast if you don't mind."

Despite telling herself to keep well in control, Felicity found her words coming out all in a rush, but as the narrative grew, she slowed down and felt more confident again.

"I have this friend, Judy. We only met up again quite recently, hadn't seen each other since we left school."

Despite his earlier avowal, Sergeant Jones interrupted with, "And how long ago would that be?"

"About ten years ago," Felicity replied. "We bumped into each other a little while ago at the market. It was Wednesday lunchtime and I had the afternoon off. I work at Mitchell and Leigh's, in the Accounts Department. When I saw her, at first I hardly knew her. She was much thinner than I remembered and her eye was badly swollen and discoloured. I would have gone by, but I saw a spark of recognition cross her face and then I recognised her, too. To cut a long story short, I invited her to my flat for the afternoon, partly to catch up on old times and partly because I sensed she was in a pretty emotional state. It was so unusual. She had always been the calm, capable type at school, clever too." She paused to sip some tea as a police constable came in. When he had left, she took a deep breath and continued.

"At first, she pretended she had bumped into a door handle, but when I made it obvious that I didn't accept that, she burst into tears and the whole story came out. She had gone to live with someone called Ron Andrews. At first he had been in a good job and was charming and attentive. Then he became redundant and although he soon found a part-time job at the Labour Club, he became moody and well, he started knocking her about."

The two interviewers looked at each other. It was an old familiar story. Again, Felicity was interrupted, this time by Constable Collier.

"I must tell you, Miss Howells," she said firmly but kindly, "that domestic violence does not become police business until the person assaulted makes a complaint herself."

"That's the point," insisted Felicity, glad of the lead in. "I don't think she's capable. I mean, I'm not sure that she's alive. Even if she is, I am certain she is being held against her will." She paused to let her words take effect.

The sergeant raised his eyebrows.

"Neither can we intervene on just speculation," he affirmed. "I presume you have grounds for this accusation?"

"Judy was bashed again yesterday. She arrived at my flat in a terrible state. Her face and neck were a mass of bruises and the skin was broken too. She looked awful – as if she had been in a terrible accident and she couldn't speak for ages. She was shaking so much. When she had calmed down she told me she was leaving him at last. She asked if she could stay at my place because she hadn't told him about meeting up with me and he wouldn't know where to find her."

She paused to take another sip.

"I pointed out that she had nothing with her. We agreed that she would go home and pack as much as she could and that she would try to get away before he came home from work. I offered to go with her, but she said she would get a taxi. She said he always went out on a Wednesday evening and she would leave the house when she was in it alone."

The Sergeant spoke again.

"I think I know what you are going to say. Your friend didn't turn up. You must understand, Miss Howells, that this is an all too common happening. Victims of abuse are often too demoralised to carry plans through, even if they've managed to make any. For some strange reason too, they are often still in love with the person assaulting them. It seems apparent that Miss Brandt simply changed her mind."

"No!" The word came out almost explosively. "She was adamant. She was afraid he would kill her. He was getting more and more out of control. She promised to ring me if she was prevented from leaving and we would try again another night. But I haven't heard a word from her. It is possible I suppose that in the end she might be too afraid to leave him, but she would definitely have let me know. I seem to be the only friend she has." Felicity mouthed a silent apology to Mel. It was important that Mel be kept out of the story for the time being, if their plan was to succeed. "Please," she urged now. "You must go round there. See if she's alright. Speak to her on her own."

Felicity allowed herself to become a little hysterical, careful not to behave in excess. For a while she was left alone. When they returned, they indicated that the interview was over. The recorder had already been switched off, but now the sergeant told her that they would go round to the given address. Their attitude was still more negative than positive, but all she wanted was for them to go round and put the fear of God into the brute who had caused her friend not just the pain, but the indignity, of being battered. She wanted them to find the small bloodstains that Judy had carefully planted from a cut finger's obliging supply. She wanted them to ask questions of the neighbours. Above all she wanted them to show enough interest to put pressure on 'that man' as she thought of him, and scare the living daylights out of him.

It was several hours before Constable Collier took a young probationer out to Lord Street and found the address given by Felicity that morning. Ron Andrews almost did not respond to the knocking at his door. He was in a state of shock and bewilderment and the stupor of too much drink. For the past two days, he had re-lived his homecoming on Wednesday, over and over again. He had come out of the shower to find the wardrobe door wide open in the bedroom. He realised at once that his box of savings had gone from the top shelf. Whilst still trying to make sense of the empty scene before him, he had turned round to the dressing table, only to register that his loose change had gone together with the roll of notes from his pocket. Without waiting to dress, he had charged down the stairs, bellowing out Judy's name, and still at a loss to understand what had happened. For the next half hour, he had searched the house, again and again, calling her name and issuing all sorts of threats, but of Judy there was no sign.

Ron had spent a long evening and even longer night trying to fathom out what had happened and why it had happened. Such was his insensitivity that he never once wondered if Judy were alright, although his first thought had been that burglars had broken in and gone off with his money. He spent a lot of time working out how he was going to manage for the rest of the month, and a good amount of time blaming Judy for allowing the burglars to get away with his tin box. It was later, after he had spat out the salty casserole that tasted so bitter, and only then did he realise that the burglars were non-existent. He could scarcely comprehend that Judy had been the thief or the following understanding that she had run away. His thoughts had been of instant revenge and he had raced upstairs to dress, and then out in the car, round and round the streets looking for her with curses and threats and useless imaginings of what he would do to her when he found her.

But he had not found her. Instead he had gone home and taken his temper out on the furniture. Now, two days later, it still lay strewn and in part, broken across the rooms. Only the lounge had remained impervious to his vandalism and he had spent most of the intervening time, slumped there, his brain too befuddled to think straight about what he was going to do. It was in this unshaven, state that he opened the door and found the two policewomen on his doorstep.

"Ron Andrews?" asked Constable Collier, politely and added at his surprised nod, "I wonder if we might come in for a moment, sir?" Without giving him time to think, she pushed past him, followed by the young probationer. Ron followed them into the lounge and beckoned for them to sit, whilst he remained standing.

"What can I do for you?" he asked belligerently. "If you've come to tell me you've found Judy and she wants to come back, you're wasting your time. I want nothing more to do with the thieving bitch."

Constable Collier looked up at the man before her. She had expected to be faced with a bull necked, heavy shouldered, swarthy individual. So much for stereotyping she thought with a wry smile, for Ron Andrews was slight, not particularly tall, and exceedingly meek and mild looking. However, she quickly noted his eyes wore a contemptuous expression and his thin mouth was already twisted into a derisive sneer. Not much respect for women police she registered.

"I take it, Sir, that you are referring to Miss Judy Brandt, who resides at this address?"

"You take it right," he snarled back. He would have said more, but the policewoman interrupted him coolly.

"You called her a thief, sir. Can you explain why?" She took out her notebook to show him that she was ready to take down anything he had to say.

Ron was totally confused.

"What the hell has that got to do with you?" he blustered. "What are you doing here anyway?"

"We have had a report that Miss Brandt has disappeared, sir. We wonder if you could throw any light on this?"

"Disappeared – no. Left – yes and good riddance. You'll probably find her swanning it up in some posh hotel, on my money. She took over six hundred pounds and when I catch up with her, I'll make the bitch suffer, I can tell you." He suddenly held himself in check as if he had said too much.

"Are you saying that you do not know where Miss Brandt is? I understand her to be your common law wife. When did you last see her? Surely she left a forwarding address for her mail and so on?"

"Look. She was here when I came home on Wednesday, early evening. I went to have a shower and when I came down, she was gone and so was my savings." He swore and leaned over the policewoman aggressively.

"I suggest we would all be more comfortable if you sat down, sir," she said, then seeing the beginning of a refusal on his lips, quickly added, "unless you would prefer that we talk down the station?"

Ron lurched into a chair. He was sobering up a little with the shock of the visit. He was however, still a little dazed by the events.

Police Constable Collier did not give him much time to think. She had come out here, half expecting to find it all the imagination of an over-zealous friend.

Now she was not so sure. She began to fire questions at him, whilst the probationer looked on and wondered if she would ever be so confident.

"You're telling us that your partner disappeared on Wednesday, without warning. You're also telling us, that rightly or wrongly, you assume she has run off of her own free will? You're also stating that she has stolen quite a large sum of money? Can you then explain why neither of these incidents have been reported to the police? I mean, how do you know she wasn't abducted? Had you any reason to think she wanted to leave home?"

Ron felt bewildered by the quickness of her words, one question coming upon another. He couldn't answer. He was trying to work out what she had asked him, when she went on.

"Was Miss Brandt not happy living with you?" she continued. "Was she perhaps fed up of you knocking her about?" Beside her, the probationer gasped.

This last query jolted his brain out of his stupor.

"Knocking her about? What do you mean? I never laid a finger on her and that's the truth. Has she said I've been knocking her about? It was probably whoever she ran off with. Gave her a black eye and went off with my money!"

"I must tell you, Mr. Andrews, that we have had no conversation with Miss Brandt. Our information comes from another source, who is a witness to some very distressing injuries to Miss Brandt's face on two occasions, the last being on Wednesday of this week, the day Miss Brandt disappeared."

Ron Andrews began to bluster, his thin face a picture of righteous indignation.

"Absolute filthy lies," he spluttered. "Filthy bloody lies and you can't prove anything different."

"Nevertheless, in view of the circumstances, perhaps you will allow us to have a look around. Miss Brandt," she added tactfully, "might have left a clue to her whereabouts that we might find. If we are able to get in touch with her, she will no longer be listed as a disappeared person." She quailed a little at what her Sergeant would say, since they had as yet no intention of putting Miss Brandt on any file, other than weekly reports.

"The sooner we look, the sooner we go," she added, and whether or not it was this last statement that made Ron Andrews agree, was not known.

"Help yourself," he said. "Don't expect me to come round with you," and he reached for a whisky bottle as they went out of the room and up the stairs.

Together the police women noted that the wardrobe still held Judy's clothes, some of them very smart, hardly the sort a woman would want to leave behind, they thought. Felicity would have been thrilled to hear them come to that conclusion. They also noticed that every room was a shambles, almost as if a struggle had gone on from room to room. Downstairs was little better, chairs overturned and cushions on the floor. In the kitchen were a pile of dirty dishes, including a casserole. On their way back to the lounge, the probationer switched on the light in the narrow corridor. Constable Collier

26

knelt down to examine some stains on the curving edge of the bottom stair. There were more stains, though very small, along the skirting of the corridor.

"Could you come out here a moment?" asked the constable and Ron Andrews shambled into the hall. "Can you explain what these are, Sir?" she asked politely.

"No I can't and I've had enough. I've got to get myself back to work for my evening shift tonight. I took yesterday off, had to go and get myself some money. Had to borrow off my brother. I can't miss my shift tonight. If you want to ask any more fool questions, you'd better come back with a warrant." He stumbled along the corridor and held the front door open as the probationer hurriedly scraped off a little of one of the stains and popped it into a page of her notebook. She didn't think they dared ask him for an envelope!

"What do you think?" she asked Constable Collier. The constable was already making her way towards the house next door. Getting no reply, she walked past Andrews' house again and went to the house on its left. This time the door opened and the lady of the house appeared as if by magic.

"I saw you go in next door," she gushed. "He hasn't killed her, has he? I knew I should have insisted on her coming in on Wednesday. Her face was in such a dreadful state and she had bruises all down her neck too. But she was so petrified of what he would do. She begged me not to let him know that I had seen her. Oh dear. Oh dear!"

Constable Collier interrupted her.

"This is certainly not a murder inquiry, Mrs.–?"

"Matthews," lisped the lady breathlessly. "I'm sorry, but if you had seen what he had done to her. Her one eye was all puffed up. You couldn't see it!"

Constable Collier decided that perhaps the best place to talk would be away from the doorstep, and all of a fuss, Mrs. Matthews led them into a comfortable, airy room, with French windows at the far end. When they were seated with the inevitable cups of tea, the constable took out her notebook and began to question Mrs. Matthews more closely. That lady, sensing the interest was a little more intense, rose to the occasion. She was genuinely concerned for her neighbour's safety, but she had to admit deep down, she was enjoying the drama of it all too.

"Now, Mrs. Matthews, you say Miss Brandt called on you on Wednesday. Could you tell us the purpose of her visit? Was she in the habit of calling on you?"

"Oh no, not really, not unless she wanted me to take in a parcel for her and that was only once, just after they moved in. Now why did she come? Oh yes, she came to warn me not to let her husband know I had seen her injuries. She was so scared of him, you see."

Something niggled at the constable's thinking and after a slight pause, she asked, "Do you mean she was asking you not to see injuries you would not have seen, had she not called round to see you? That's a bit Irish isn't it?" She apologised mentally to her Irish grandfather.

"No, not at all. Well I mean, I wouldn't have seen them if she hadn't have knocked, but she wasn't referring to Wednesday's err –" she strained to find the right word, "- err, battering."

"She wasn't?" queried a rather confused constable.

"No. I had seen her before, more than once, usually when she was in the garden. I would watch out for her," she indicated the French windows, "and sometimes I would just catch her hanging out the washing, but she often disappeared indoors as soon as she saw me – didn't want me to see her like that. But one day I persevered and gave up pretending I hadn't see the state she was in. I asked if I could help in any way, and why didn't she leave."

"But this was the first time, she had actually called round and brought the subject up herself?" persisted the policewoman.

Mrs. Matthews nodded.

"Yes, because this time she seemed really terrified. She was shaking you know."

The niggle faded away. Everything seemed to fit. Taking Mrs. Matthews through her account just once again, she thanked her and advised her to keep away from her neighbour Mr. Andrews and leave everything to the police.

"It may well be that Miss Brandt had taken your advice and run away," she said as they left, "we'll find her soon I'm sure." But she didn't really think so and neither did the probationer or Mrs. Matthews.

Back at the police station, they made their report to the sergeant, who took them to see the Inspector. He listened carefully to what they had to say.

"Well, what is your opinion?" he asked at last.

"At first, sir, I must admit I thought Miss Howells was probably getting stirred up over little more than a battering, not that that isn't serious enough. But his story was so weird, her running out on him whilst he was in the shower. Why didn't she go before he came home, and why cook a casserole for him?" She blushed as she realised she could have brought the dish to investigate the strange bitter taste Ron Andrews had mentioned. "We also found some stains, small but they look like reasonably fresh bloodstains to me. Young Bellingham has gone down to the lab with a few scrapings, sir." She was glad that they had at least thought to do that.

Inspector Graham pushed back his chair and stood with his back to them for a while.

"Alright, constable, leave it with me for now. You may go but there is something I'd like to discuss with you, Sergeant Jones, if you would kindly stay another moment."

The policewoman left, a flush appearing in her cheeks. She guessed that her credibility was being questioned and as it turned out, she was right.

"Well Sergeant, do you think the constable is over re-acting because we are dealing with violence against a woman, or not? Give me your honest opinion."

"In this case, sir, I think the constable genuinely believes there is something to investigate and I must say I agree with her. For one thing, she was quite sceptical at first. She expected to find Miss Brandt at home and vowing that she had walked into the door or the like. As a rule, she is very level headed and professional, sir, otherwise she wouldn't be getting her promotion through so soon."

"Well then, we'd better keep her on the case and you'd both better do some more serious digging. Go and see the complainant again too. See if she comes up with anything more specific and have a word with the manager of the Club where Andrews works. But at this stage, be discreet. We don't want to give an innocent man grounds for complaint against us."

"Right, sir," said the sergeant, and taking himself to be dismissed, he left the room.

PART THREE

The next few days were becoming a nightmare for Ron. For one thing, he was beginning to miss Judy. He missed having her at his beck and call. He missed having his meals ready and waiting, his shirts washed and neatly pressed, and he had to admit, he missed her for herself. Finding the whisky bottles all empty one morning, for once he sat down and allowed his head to clear a little. He was on late shift and did not have to be at the Club until six-thirty. So he sat and thought wryly. Where had she gone? Had anything happened to her? Had she been abducted? If so, why? And if not, why too? Try as he might, he could not rid himself of the answer to why she would have gone. He had hit her, far too often and lately, far too hard. For the first time, guilt weighed heavily on his conscience and he found himself feeling upset, genuinely upset by his behaviour. Several times he would shake his head and ask himself why he had hit her and try hard to think back to why he had hit her the very first time. He had been very sorry immediately then and had vowed never to lay a finger on her again. But he had, and now he didn't know why and wished she were here for him to say sorry.

The sun began to weaken outside and still he sat on. He was frightened now. Would he be able to control himself next time? Would he be lashing out at her for the rest of her life? If she was still alive.

"Judy," he moaned, "come home. I'll never harm you again. I'll even give up the drink, if that's what you'd like," but even as he made this last committal, he knew he could never keep to that. He had been drinking since he was sixteen. He couldn't stop now. The thought depressed him further as he looked at the clock and decided he should get ready for work.

Although on reaching the Club, he began to drink steadily, for once he found his spirits did not lift at all. For one thing, people seemed to be behaving rather oddly towards him. Bob, the Manager had been far too hearty and had seemed embarrassed somehow. The customers were not so eager to prop up the bar either and those who did, avoided eye contact and seemed to be talking unnaturally loudly. He tried to tell himself it was imagination, but he guessed that word of Judy's disappearance was getting round. He had kept Judy well away from the Club, preferring her to stay in at home. He didn't like the idea of other men ogling her.

It suddenly dawned on him that perhaps the police were going round asking questions. They had been back to the house once, asking about the casserole dish, but he had washed it and put it away. Did they really think he had done away with her? Was that what they were thinking? Throughout the evening, he served mechanically, his thoughts going round and round trying to remember if the police had in any way intimated that he was guilty of something more than domestic bashing, but they had been very polite.

Other thoughts disturbed him now. Had they been bothering the neighbours, the shopkeepers, the postman, the bin men, the paper boy even? Perspiration broke out on his forehead, and he was glad to find himself out in the open air away from people as his shift ended.

That night, he could not sleep. He cleaned the house from top to bottom. It was four in the morning before he flopped onto the settee and even though he was weary, he tossed about in fitful dozing. When morning came, he was stiff and cramped and more tired than ever.

Meanwhile the police were stepping up their inquiries. Several tradesmen and callers at the house had affirmed the evidence of a pattern of injuries. Some had looked away. The postman had asked if Judy had needed help. But the hands of the police were tied without a complaint from the lady herself. Inspector Graham decided they should step up the pressure and try to manoeuvre a confession, so ten days after Judy's disappearance, they began to make several calls at the house.

The first visit was early Sunday morning. Ron was half awake, unshaven and suffering a hangover. It took him half an hour to register that they obviously suspected him of being responsible for Judy's absence.

"Look, it's my fault she's gone. I know it," he cried. "I drove her to it. I was too handy with my fists. But she left of her own accord. Her going was a complete shock to me."

On the second visit on the same day, the police referred to information received from Judy's female friend, which indicated that she had promised to leave him and go and stay a while with her, but she had not turned up.

"What friend? Judy had no friends, only me. She never went out except for food and things like that. I wouldn't let her go out to work and more often than not, I would be out shopping with her. If she had a friend, I would have known about it."

The next day, three policemen arrived on his doorstep. Mrs. Matthews was almost permanently seated behind her lace curtains now and she spent a long time on the phone, seemingly giving running commentaries, with suitable embellishments presumably, since all she could see was someone going in and then someone coming out.

This time Ron was becoming more and more frightened and more belligerent.

"Take me to this 'female friend'. I'll soon get her to change her story. It's lies. All lies," he bellowed, fear making him splutter.

The lady in question is highly respected in the community," mentioned Sergeant Jones that afternoon. "We are convinced her story is true and her concern for Miss Brandt is sincere."

Ron was gradually being worn down. He was so tired he could not seem to get his thoughts together enough to think what he should do. It was the police who suggested he might get in touch with a solicitor. Had the idea come from himself he might have felt relieved, but coming from them brought him renewed terror. He felt himself being drawn into a net, from which he could not see any escape. But he did not actually begin to shake until they arrived on the Thursday afternoon and announced that they were going to dig up the garden. Thereafter, he could only slump helplessly into his armchair and let the activity go on around him, barely conscious of who was speaking to him or of what the people going back and forward through his house, were doing.

About this time, Felicity was beginning to find the strain quite unnerving. She had been told by the police that they were going to dig up the garden, and the enormity of her part in the deceit was beginning to dawn. The three women had planned everything so carefully, but they had not considered the cost to the taxpayers of any activity such as digging up gardens. She decided the time to act had come.

A message came through to Sergeant Jones, whilst he was actually supervising the removal of some flagstones.

"It's Miss Howells, sir. She said it's urgent. She says she's heard from Miss Brandt, sir."

The excitement of the young officer got through to the inspector rather than the words themselves. He gave an abrupt signal for everyone to take a rest and took up the 'phone.

"Oh, inspector. It's wonderful. It's all been a misunderstanding. Judy and Mel have just rung me!" She did not say she had rung them from first. She held her breath and waited for the explosion, but the inspector spoke quite calmly.

"I'm very glad to hear that, Miss Howells. Who might this Mel be?"

"She's my best friend and you see she's only just rung. She's got Judy with her and they didn't know she was supposed to be missing and –" the Inspector cut her short.

I think you'd better make your way to the station and I will meet you there." He put the phone down abruptly. He was glad they had barely begun any serious digging. Everything was easily replaceable. Calling the Sergeant over, he cautioned him to keep Mr. Andrews distracted whilst they repaired any damage immediately.

"He's not off the hook yet though," he advised. "There's no knowing with this silly woman. She might have got this information wrong too."

Twenty minutes later, the inspector was sitting facing Felicity in the same interview room that Sergeant Jones and Constable Collier had listened to her initial complaint. By now his veneer of politeness was wearing a little thin as the full implications of waste in terms of time, money and workforce registered. He was therefore a little abrupt, acknowledging her presence with barely a nod. He put on the tape and indicated he was waiting for her to speak.

Felicity had no need of polite chit chat. She was too anxious to get this, the hardest part over.

"Inspector. This afternoon, I had a call from my friend Mel. She lives just along the corridor from me in Flat 14. I said "Cheerio" to her last Wednesday as she was off on her holidays, going down to Penarth in South Wales to stay in her uncle's holiday home. Well apparently, she bumped into Judy down in the basement. I had just gone off to see what had happened to Judy. I was in a bit of a state because she hadn't turned up and I thought I would drive a little way along and look for her. I thought perhaps her taxi hadn't turned up for her. I guess I was too restless just to hang about waiting, so I thought I'd look out for her. Well, when she bumped into Mel, she was apparently in a terrible state, almost incoherent, but Mel managed to find out that Judy was heading for my flat. They both came back up in the lift only to find my flat was empty."

The inspector interrupted as she drew breath.

"Your friend had a key to your flat?"

"Yes, just as I have a key to hers. We let ourselves in and out all the time."

The inspector sighed.

"Go on, Miss Howells." He showed no sign of softening. Felicity went on nervously.

"Mel says Judy was in such a state she didn't want to leave her. Then Judy started worrying that her Ron Andrews might have followed her to the flat and then

Mel began worrying about what he might do to me if he found Judy there. So, just on the spur of the moment as it were, Mel decided the best thing all round would be for Judy to go down to Wales with her, and – and that's what happened." Her voice tailed off lamely as she realised the thinness of her story.

The inspector said nothing and the silence hung in the air between them. Felicity was tempted to gabble on, but an inner voice told her to stay calm and say nothing more. Eventually, the inspector spoke, weighing his words carefully.

"You're telling me, that your friend took Miss Brandt away on holiday for a fortnight, without telling you what she had done?" His tone showed his disbelief. His mind was trying to unravel the reasons this lady should be lying to him. He decided to let her talk on, and maybe she would tie herself into knots.

"Oh no, inspector. That's just it. She scribbled me a note and she left it tucked inside the Horlicks jar. She knows I always have Horlicks before going to bed and she thought it would be safer there than on the table or somewhere where it could get blown away."

This time the Inspector's sigh was even deeper and heavy with sarcasm.

"Really."

Felicity hurried on. She wished that they had acted this part out. Then they might have been aware of how flimsy their story was when presented to hard-hearted police officers. She tried to appear earnest and sincere and extremely apologetic and anxious to please.

"But you see, I was so upset and worried that I decided not to have Ovaltine. My tummy seemed too churned up so I settled for a cup of tea, and that's what I've been drinking ever since. So I never found the note and I didn't know." She decided that this time she had really said enough. Now it was for the inspector to be convinced of her deep regret for wasting time. She looked at him appealingly, unashamedly using her femininity.

The inspector hardly knew what to think. Either she was a consummate actress, or she really was as helpless and innocent as she appeared. His first instinct was to dismiss her story as total invention, yet experience had taught him that truth was often presented in a more fantastic way than fiction. Any motive for intervention on her part escaped him. He left the room for a while and on his return asked her for a written statement, telling her in the same abrupt way, that she could go when it was finished and signed.

Felicity left the station feeling quite deflated. She had not envisaged the strain of maintaining her story in the presence of a man who was obviously most professional and quite astute. Whether or not he believed her, she had no idea.

By the time she had reached the flat, her spirits rose again. Mel had told her that away from Ron Andrews, Judy had shown remarkable resilience. She was making plans for her future in which he would definitely have no part, and her gratitude to the two friends was strongly evident.

That weekend, when the three friends were drinking Ovaltine at Felicity's flat, they expressed their satisfaction.

Everything had gone very much to plan. Although Judy had not pressed charges, Ron Andrews had been in turn bewildered, angry, disturbed and finally ostracised by his workmates. His neighbours refused to speak to him. For ten days he had been accused of being a murderer. Judy's reappearance might remove the stigma of being called 'murderer', but the whole town was aware of the reasons for her disappearance. Already, Judy had been approached by the news media and had not hesitated to offer them clear accounts of the dreadful abuse she had suffered for so long. Although she had been factual rather than inventive, Felicity and Mel had already reasoned that the details once published would appear in a much more lurid and dramatic form. Revenge would be sweet indeed.

That night, in Felicity's spare bedroom, Judy lay awake. She was aware that she did not quite share her friends' euphoria. Poor Ron. She felt sorry for him. They had gone too far. He would probably have to leave the town where he had lived all his life. All his friends had turned against him. He needed her now, more than ever. If she went to him, after a little time had passed, perhaps…

THE WRONG GIRL

PART ONE

The girl in the red coat was hurrying along the tree-lined lane in the greyness of early evening. She heard a vehicle crunching behind her on the gravel, but she did not hear the footsteps. Just as she began to move over to give the van passing room, the gloom of dusk turned rapidly into blackness, as a sack was thrown over her head and two muscular arms grabbed her from behind. Before she was really aware of what was happening, she found herself being thrust into the back of a van. Still shocked, she was bewildered to feel a fairly gentle pat on her shoulder from someone inside with her. Then the vehicle's doors closed with a loud clash of metal and the van moved off.

Lucy could neither think nor feel. She lay on the floor, stunned and immobile. It was a few minutes before she felt an ache in her side and back from the jolting of the van as it bumped along the lane. It was days later before she was to realize, that what was happening to her was all down to the three 'ifs'.

If there had not been a patient needing urgent attention to his teeth, delaying her for half an hour; if she had not needed to hurry home to be there when her partner Chris was due to ring her from his holiday chalet in Switzerland and if she had not decided to use the lane as a short cut, she would not have found herself in such a dangerous situation!

But, for the present, her senses were only slowly coming back to her, although it was not long before she became more vividly aware of what was happening to her. The sack over her face was uncomfortably stuffy. She could hardly breathe. She had no idea of why she had been taken, or by whom, but instinct told her to lie still as if she had fainted, even as she felt her hands being tied by fraying rope. Slowly, fear took over and she lay there, uncomprehending and filled with dread.

She thought she must have fainted, because the next sound she heard was a gruff voice, coming from whoever was driving.

"We've got her, Guv, all tied up and nowhere to go." Then there was silence. She guessed he was using his phone and now, listening to someone. Then she almost moved with a start, as there came a startled, "What? Are you sure? How do you know?"

Through the sacking, she heard muffled cursing. Then the van came to a lurching halt that made Lucy roll onto her side. She kept as unmoving as she could as the van doors opened and an angry discussion took place between the driver and her attacker.

"What's up?" asked the latter.

"We have only gone and picked the wrong girl," answered the driver gruffly. "Guv's seen the target letting herself into her home. He is not pleased."

"Well, it is not our fault. This girl was in the right place at the right time and she was wearing a red coat. What do we do now?"

"Has she seen your face?" asked his accomplice.

"No. I grabbed her from behind and put the sack over her head straight away. Besides, I think she fainted as soon as she was in the van."

"Good," grunted the driver. "We don't want to go down for murder. We'll dump her on the grass verge. Someone will find her soon enough. Then we'll get away from here sharpish and wait for further orders from the guy who's paying us."

So both men pulled her up into a sitting position and clumsily dropped her onto the roadside. As she fell, Lucy gave a gasp of pain as her head hit a sharp stone.

"She is coming to," muttered her attacker. "Let's get going."

Lucy felt nothing more until she awoke to find herself in hospital. Her head hurt and putting up a hand to touch it, she realized both her head and her right hand were bandaged. Not yet fully conscious, she sensed that someone was sitting beside her bed, but a misty haze swam before her eyes and she could not focus properly. She heard voices and slowly turned her head. She sensed someone leaning over her as a cool hand stroke her cheek.

Lucy sensed it was a nurse as a voice softly murmured, "Just relax, my dear. You are in hospital, but you will soon be feeling much better. Later on, the police will want to ask you some questions, only to help you," she added as Lucy stirred uneasily. "but for now, try to rest."

The gentle voice was soothing and Lucy felt safe and was soon fast asleep.

It was hours later before she awoke, her mouth dry and her head throbbing unpleasantly. This time she could see it was a young policeman at her bedside. He held a glass of water in his hand and lifted her head very gently so that she could take a sip.

"Do you think you could answer a few questions, now?" he asked.

Lucy did not know. What questions could she possibly answer? Still, she whispered, "I'll try."

The policeman leaned forward and smiled at her encouragingly.

"Can you tell us what happened?" he asked in a kind, concerned voice.

"I don't know. Why am I here? Am I ill?" she whispered. She felt totally confused.

"You were found near a ditch on Kerslake Road. Your head was bleeding and you had a sack over it. Your hands were tied in front of you, but not too tightly, but they had scraped against something sharp. Can you remember anything at all?"

Lucy shook her head slowly. Nothing made sense as she struggled to think.

"The wrong girl," she sighed drowsily, "the wrong girl."

As the nurse came back into the ward in time to hear the last sleepy words, she indicated that he should try again the next day. So after checking that his relief had arrived to be on guard outside Lucy's room all night, the policeman reported back to his sergeant at the police station.

"The only thing she said, Sarge, was 'the wrong girl'. She must have been thrown down roughly to hit her head on that stone so hard and she was barely conscious. There were no other significant injuries, just a few scrapes on her hands."

"The 'wrong girl' – that's a puzzle. Who was the right girl, I wonder? Was someone else the intended victim?" He pondered for a moment or so, before coming to a decision.

"We will leave it to the detectives from now on, but we will keep a constable on guard until the plain clothes squad takes over. There is nothing else that we can do, for now."

PART TWO:
THE INVESTIGATION BEGINS.

Detective Inspector Rogerson sighed. He had read through the notes before him several times during the last two days. There had been little advancement, although the girl had been identified as Lucy James, a young dental nurse. Enquiries at the surgery where she worked and at the flat where she lived with her boyfriend Chris, suggested that she was an ordinary, hard-working, friendly girl. Her friends had expressed amazement that she had been temporarily abducted and they intended to visit the hospital frequently to offer support. Hopefully, their visits would help her memory to return. So far, she did remember leaving the surgery late and taking a short cut to get home in time for a phone call from Switzerland, where Chris and his fellow mates from his architect's office were on a skiing trip.

'Time is of the essence,' thought Rogerson. Aloud, he said, "The attacker could be miles away by now and we have nothing to go on. Oak Tree Lane leads to just two large houses at its end. One has been turned into flats by the owner, who lives next door in the other. Apparently, he is wealthy and spends much of his time abroad, where he is at present. His house is therefore unoccupied, so we will begin our enquiries at the flats. Lucy's boyfriend is returning on the first flight he can get. He will want to go straight to the hospital, but we will speak with him as soon as we can."

These remarks were directed at his young probationer. Detective Constable Fulford was nodding in agreement, but for some reason, having only just met her, Rogerson thought she seemed a little scatty. He hoped she would prove useful though and shortly afterwards, she was following him into the top apartment of a large, imposing house at the end of Oak Tree Lane. They were ushered into a large, expensively decorated room, with a stupendous view of the hills beyond. Every piece of furniture spoke of wealth and good taste.

The man who had invited them in, was tall and good looking. He had an air of confidence, arrogance even, but offered the policeman and police woman coffee, graciously enough. Emerging from another room, was an equally tall, elegant young woman, who offered them both her hand, before sitting on a low, comfortable-looking settee. Soon, the man returned with cups of steaming coffee and introduced himself and his wife as Gavin and Libby Brooks.

After a few pleasantries, Rogerson explained the reason for their visit.

"You may have heard that a young woman from the ground floor flat here, was kidnapped at the far end of this lane two days ago?"

Husband and wife nodded solemnly. Rogerson continued, "Her hands were tied, a sack placed over head and she was dumped a few miles away, on the side of a busy road. Unfortunately, she cannot recall much about the attack. We are wondering if you have seen any strangers loitering about here recently."

Both looked shocked as they shook their heads, frowning as if trying to remember. Then Gavin Brooks held up a finger as if something had suddenly come to mind.

"Well, come to think of it, I did see a white van passing once or twice. It was rather shabby, which is probably why I noticed it," he added, somewhat snobbishly.

His wife Libby looked at him silently. She appeared rather nervous and seeing the detectives looking her way, she spoke in a high, clear voice.

"I have not had the police in my home before and I must confess it is an unsettling experience." She smiled self-consciously and blushed.

When the detectives left a few minutes later, D.C Fulford was thinking that she would have to work late again as she breathed, "Another dead end, sir."

Her boss nodded and they went down a curving staircase to the second floor, where two flats shared a landing. The detectives had already learned that the elderly couple from 2A were away, so they made straight for Flat 2B, where they were introduced to a young couple whose names turned out to be Mick and Julie Watkins.

Refusing the offer of a drink, both detectives noticed that by comparison with the apartment upstairs, the room they entered was much shabbier. The furniture looked worn and the ornaments were tatty. Both occupants wore threadbare jeans and none too clean T shirts. Mick sported lurid scrawls of tattoo designs up both his arms, whilst his finger tips bore evidence of heavy smoking.

As they sat down, Mick spoke. "I saw that you visited upstairs first," he grunted, "so you must think our flat very different from that of her 'High and Mighty Libby Brooks,' not to mention 'Oh, So Posh' Gavin!"

D.I. Rogerson did not offer a conciliatory response, but instead asked a question.

"Why the nicknames and why the tone of dislike?" he asked.

It was Julie who answered. "Libby is the daughter of the owner of this house and the house next door where he lives, when he is not swanning off abroad. The Brooks live rent-free and think themselves better than the likes of us, who pay our rent regularly and have to work hard for what we have, when we can get work, that is," she snorted. "We are both currently out of work since the local factory closed and 'him upstairs' is always looking down his nose at us."

D.I.Rogerson sympathized. Something was niggling at the back of his mind, but it was nothing to do with snobbery. For some reason, he had taken a dislike to the Brooks couple, but he could not yet fathom why.

Instead his thoughts turned to the present company.

'Could this young couple be poor enough to try and kidnap someone? Could Libby, whose father was obviously of substantial wealth, have been the 'Right Girl' He looked at Mick's stocky build and thought he would have been strong enough to lift someone into a van.'

But he did not voice these thoughts whirling round in his rather oversized head and having gained no useful information, he left the flat with his probationer D.C. Fulford following him.

As they descended the stairs, he asked her if she thought Mick Watkins could be a suspect. Her reply astonished him.

"Oh no, sir. Did you notice he had nice dimples? People with dimples are always good-natured, friendly sorts."

D.I.Rogerson groaned in disbelief. "You want to get out more, lass," was all he allowed himself to say.

Their next call was at Flat 1B. The door opened at the first ring and a dour man in paint-smudged overalls, let them in. Introducing himself as Tom Crocker, he beckoned them into a bright, cosy living room. Again there was an offer of a drink, which again was politely declined. There was no sign of a Mrs. Crocker, but a young man strolled into the room with a suspicious nod and sat opposite them.

"This is my son, Ben." growled Tom, his voice naturally deep and gravelly. "You will need to be quick as he is due to work the evening shift at the High Street Restaurant, soon."

"Do you work every evening, sir?" asked D.I. Rogerson politely.

"Yes, apart from Wednesdays and Sundays," replied Ben, a now eager to please expression crossing his chubby face.

Wednesday was the evening Lucy had been attacked and both detectives made the same mental note. They explained the reason for their visit, but the older man interrupted them quickly.

"Yes, we heard about it," he assured them, "but I don't think we can be of any help. I was out decorating a house in mill Street until about eight o'clock. I stayed late because the people were in a hurry to move in and wanted it finished."

"Is there a Mrs. Crocker?" asked Fulford, although she guessed there was. The flowery wallpaper suggested a woman's touch.

"Yes," both men answered together. Tom then went

on to say that she was working at a hairdressing salon. "My wife is very friendly with Lucy and she is upset and worried about how Lucy is. We hope those responsible are found quickly. I can't imagine how her partner Chris must be feeling, being so far away when it happened. As for Lucy, we are hoping the shock will cushion her somehow, until she is back home with Chris to look after her."

Since neither man could recall seeing anything suspicious, the detectives left. Once outside the door, D.I. Rogerson thoughtfully commented that the son had not been at work on the Wednesday, but his probationer announced cheerfully that she was sure that he was innocent.

"Ben is a name that suggests a warm and compassionate person," she asserted, with no idea of how ridiculous that sounded to her superior, a man who based his assumptions on observation, availability and instinct.

"Words fail me," was his only comment, but the shrug of his shoulders in disbelief. As they neared the door to Flat 1A, it opened. Waiting there was an anxious looking stocky, fair haired man, tanned from his trip. He greeted them impatiently.

"Come in. I saw your car outside and I expected you to come to our flat first. I paid a quick visit to the hospital, but promised Lucy I would soon be back to stay with her. She is looking very frail."

As they entered another bright and airy room, D.C. Fulford explained that they were giving him time to unpack. As expected, Chris had no information to offer. Visibly upset, he begged them to find out who had taken her and why and to apprehend them as soon as possible.

"Her memory is returning slowly though the inspector and the ward sister asked me to tell you that Lucy does now remember being bundled into a van."

"Well, sir, that is encouraging. We shall be visiting the hospital later this evening. Anything new she can tell us will be of help. We too want to make an arrest as soon as possible."

As they took their leave, the inspector wondered what idiotic comment his assistant might come up with this time. He was not to be disappointed.

"He is in the clear, sir. Did you notice his face was covered with freckles beneath that tan. Freckles for friendliness," she added.

"And there was I about to infer that he could well have set someone up to attack Lucy whilst he was conveniently away," grinned Rogerson wryly with a disbelieving shake of his head.

"How long have you been a probationer detective, Fulford?" he asked.

"Two months, sir," she replied.

"You have er remarkably intuitive ideas," he sighed.

"I take that as a compliment, sir. Thank you," she responded, oblivious to his sarcasm.

Rogerson gave a resigned sigh and said no more as they made their way back to the police station.

PART THREE: THE RIGHT GIRL.

The next day, D.I.Rogerson and his probationer met together in his office with D.S.Newbold, so that the three of them could bounce ideas of each other, although secretly the D.I. hoped that his young protégé would stay silent. Newbold had been filled in with all the details, including one new piece of evidence resulting from the visit to the hospital the previous evening. Lucy was now recovering well and was at last able to describe everything that had happened to her. She had also been able to tell them that three men were involved and recited what she could remember about the telephone conversation between the driver and someone he called 'Guv', which had resulted in her being identified as the 'wrong girl' and being dumped at the roadside.

All three men were well acquainted with the 'wrong girl' scenario now, so the focal point of the meeting was to ponder over what had prompted the men to pick up Lucy.

It was the sergeant who pointed out the relevance of Lucy being later leaving work than usual. It was decided that they should keep watch near the turn-off to the lane, to see if any woman regularly used that route at that time of early evening. So they deployed colleagues to be positioned at vantage points every evening for the rest of the week, ensuring that two Wednesdays were covered. It was to no avail.

Meanwhile, three men were meeting at a car park in the town centre. The smartly dressed man did most of the talking, whilst the two rougher looking chaps nodded now and again, obviously receiving new orders. Then they went their separate ways, the talker returning to a car, being driven by a woman.

They drove home in silence. The man was wondering if it really was a clever ruse to follow the original plan so soon after the first had failed. The woman's thoughts might have surprised him, but they were of one mind about one thing.

"You look so attractive in that red coat. Perhaps you should wear it more often, darling." He grinned and she smiled in return and were chuckling quietly as they reached home.

PART FOUR:
THE BEST LAID PLANS.

It was the second Wednesday after Lucy had been attacked and she was at home at last. Chris had hovered over her throughout the day before, but all she really wanted was to be left alone. She found that being fussed over made her feel helpless and she was determined to get back to normal as soon as possible. So this morning, she had sent him off to work, assuring him that she would keep the phone by her side and would ring the office if she needed him.

Now she sat looking out of the window at the sunshine, enjoying being away from the hospital. She waved to her neighbour from upstairs as Julie set off, probably to the Job Centre. Idly, she wondered if the 'right girl' could be someone she knew. She was the only nurse at the dental surgery. She knew Tom usually drove Stella to work when he could and that Libby normally drove herself when going out, although sometimes, she had walked. None of the women in the flats looked like her, anyway.

Lucy was just about to dismiss the idea that the intended victim could have been one of her neighbours, when a thought came to her. Hadn't one of her attackers mentioned a coat, yes, a red coat! She caught her breath as she recalled seeing one of those who shared this house, leaving this morning wearing a red coat. It was not quite the same colour or indeed, shape as hers, but it was red. The more she thought about it, the more sure she became. She must warn her neighbour's husband. She had not seen him leave yet.

Lucy struggled to her feet, realizing how weak she was, but determined to be able to climb the stairs. This she did very slowly, hanging onto the stair rail to heave herself up.

Meanwhile, D.I.Rogerson was having a few thoughts of his own. Why was it that the only ones who had seemed sympathetic to Lucy's plight, were the Crockers? Why had the Watkins been more interested in the neighbours above them? Why was Gavin Brookes the only one to have spotted a strange van in the lane?

Looking at the calendar confirmed it was Wednesday again. Should he have kept up the surveillance? Surely, the men would not be daft enough to try again, same place, same time? Not a man with friendly freckles or dimples or a homely name like Ben, he chuckled. But another thought quickly followed. It was the action of an arrogant man, just the sort of trick Gavin might try, scoffing at the stupidity of the police!

Quickly, he made a decision. It was early morning and he had plenty of time to round up his sergeant and flannel headed Fulford, but first, he wanted to check that Lucy was safe at home with Chris.

Rogerson dialed Lucy's number and waited impatiently for a reply. There was none. Perhaps Chris had taken her out for a drive? He decided to ring Chris's office, just to make sure he had not been called in to work as he knew the architects were very busy now, planning a new project of some magnitude. All the same, he was disappointed to hear Chris answer his call.

"I was hoping you would be home with Lucy today," said the D.I.

"Why? Has anything happened?" asked the worried young man. "Lucy said she didn't want me fussing over her and insisted that I came into the office," he explained hurriedly.

"Nothing's happened. It is just that she is not answering her phone," the D.I. answered. He did not want to alarm Chris by saying that his partner might be alone with a kidnapper. However Chris was alarmed to hear Lucy wasn't answering her phone and said he would be going straight home.

Rogerson rang his team and told them to drop whatever they were doing and meet him near the turn off to the lane. He would be going to the flats first to check on Lucy. He did not voice his suspicions. Instead. he concentrated on getting to the other end of the lane first. As he turned his car into the drive at the front of the house, he had a strong feeling that he would not find Lucy in her flat. Trusting his instincts, when he reached the door of 1A, he did not linger after ringing the bell twice, but began to hurry towards the stairs.

Startled, he turned to find a breathless Chris entering the main door and watched as Chris let himself into the flat.

"Come with me, son," he urged and Chris followed without hesitation, unquestionably. They raced up the stairs together.

PART FIVE:
THE SECOND ATTEMPT.

Meanwhile, Lucy had reached the top apartment at last. She was surprised to see how breathless she was and stood outside on the landing, waiting to get her breath back. She wanted to warn Gavin that his wife might have been the intended victim, but now, she was thinking her reason was flimsy. She stood outside the door, undecided and had determined to leave well alone, when the door burst open and Gavin came hurrying out. He stopped short in surprise, when he saw her.

"Er, Lucy, isn't it?" he mumbled, "I thought you were still in hospital. Are you alright?"

"It may sound foolish," spoke Lucy in a rush, "but it has occurred to me that your wife has a red coat, not unlike mine and she might have been mistaken for me, from the back, that is," she added, "when I was attacked, you know."

Gavin stood there looking down at her. Something in his eyes made her feel uneasy, but before she could turn away, Gavin had pulled her not too gently, inside the apartment. Seeing the alarm on her face, he hastened to reassure her.

"Sorry if I frightened you, Lucy, but I must make an urgent call. I will take on board what you are saying, I assure you, but I must make a call first. Do sit down. You look exhausted. I won't be more of a minute or two." Then he went quickly into the next room, closing the door firmly after him.

Lucy sat obediently, thinking how naïve she must have sounded, stupid even. Gavin was speaking urgently into his phone, his voice no more than a whisper.

"Cancel everything, now, at once!" he ordered.

"Can't do, Guv," a voice replied. "I've just got her into the van and – what the…?" The gruff voice had finished with a startled shout. Gavin clutched the phone and listened to the shouting and swearing that came down the line and knew everything had gone wrong. But he would not be going to prison, of that he was certain.

Dropping the phone, he rushed back into the other room, grabbing a briefcase and a pre-packed small hand case and in less than a minute, he had hustled a bewildered Lucy out of the apartment.

"We have to go, Lucy. The police have just warned me to get you safely away from here. There has been another attack, but my wife is safe. We will have to go out of the back way. I will explain as we go along."

"But where are we going?" asked Lucy, who was now totally confused, "I must ring Chris. I must ring Chris!" she repeated in a half wail.

Then she heard her partner's voice. "There is no need, darling. I am already here and I am not alone!"

Relief flooded over her as she saw that their way was being blocked by not only Chris but D.I. Rogerson himself. Gavin turned around, desperately, but found his way blocked by several uniformed policemen.

He gave a resigned sigh and let himself be led away into a waiting police van, already occupied by his two scowling accomplices.

PART SIX: EXPLANATIONS.

The next afternoon, Chris and Lucy were ushered into a room at the police station, where they found the three detectives waiting for them.

"Is it all over?" asked Lucy.

"We think so," replied Rogerson, "but if Gavin Brooks is to be believed, it is motivated by greed as most of these kidnappings are. It appears that Gavin has been dissatisfied living in an apartment, when his father-in-law owns property both here and abroad. Libby's father had refused to subsidise the young couple's extravagant tastes. He regards giving them the apartment as an adequate gesture. He is a self-made man and expected his son-in-law to maintain his wife, as any honest hard-working man would,

"Gavin had other ideas?" asked Chris.

"Yes. He hit on a plan to have Libby kidnapped for a sizeable ransom. She was not to be hurt but to be bundled into the van roughly enough to convince any passers-by that might have come along, that it was a serious assault. He was sure his father-in-law would pay to have her released and she was then to be returned unharmed. Gavin would have the bulk of the ransom money, but the two men would also be well recompensed.

"How was Gavin going to be able to explain his new wealth?" asked Chris.

"A fair point," replied the D.I. "but he was going to let a few months pass and then claim to have found a well paid executive post somewhere."

"I was right then. He must have persuaded his wife to wear a red coat. That was to be how they would recognize the victim in the half light," sighed Lucy, thinking she would never wear her coat again.

"Do you think, she was in it with him?" asked D.C. Fulford.

'Wow,' thought D.I. Rogerson. 'A sensible question from my probationer. Thing are looking up !'

"Well it appears that Lucy was not meant to be harmed. The men panicked when they realized their mistake," mused Sergeant Newbold.

"Are you saying that Gavin Brooks loves his wife, that he just wanted more money?" asked Chris.

"It would appear so. I watched him saying goodbye to his wife before entering a holding cell last night. I don't think he wanted her to be charged and was apologizing as if she were not involved in any way. He wanted to protect her and take all the blame on himself. Either she is innocent or she is a good actress, for she appeared to be in shock, as any victim would have been," replied D.I.Rogerson, rather cautiously.

"He will go to prison?" asked D.C.Fulford.

'There goes the sensible questions,' smiled D.I. to himself before replying with a straight face, "Yes, but attempted kidnap would not have resulted in a serious sentence, had he not succeeded in kidnapping Lucy, first. He should go down for a few years together with the men he had promised to pay."

Just as Lucy and Chris were about to leave, Lucy turned back.

"Inspector Rogerson, what was it that made you suspect Gavin in the end?"

"Well," he smiled, "you see it couldn't have been a man with dimples, or freckles or a people friendly name like Ben, could it?" He winked at D.C. Fulford, who had the grace to blush, leaving Chris and Lucy to try to work out what was obviously a joke of some kind!

PART SEVEN: DOUBTS.

That night, Rogerson found himself unable to sleep. Now that the case had been solved, he had expected to sleep through the night, but after tossing and turning, he got up and went downstairs to his study. Sighing, he poured himself a whisky and sat at his desk, mulling over all that had happened that day. What had he missed? Whatever it was, it continued to elude him, so he went back to bed and this time fell into a deep sleep.

In the morning, his wife let him sleep on, but to her amazement, at nine o'clock, he rushed down the stairs, kissed her on the forehead and dashed out to his car. From past experience, she guessed he had a hunch about something and she shook her head, wonderingly.

Arriving at the police station, Rogerson surprised his sergeant by asking him to arrange an appointment at the prison, saying no more than that he needed to speak with Gavin Brooks again. He informed his sergeant that he would need him and his new rather dizzy D.C. Fulford to accompany him.

Ten minutes later, they were speeding away. Newbold and Fulford sat in silence, knowing better than to ask questions, but eventually he broke the silence.

"Something about the meeting between Gavin and his wife yesterday is troubling me. I can't lay a finger on it, but I need to see him again."

With that, they had to be content.

They were ushered into an empty visiting room of the prison which took the overflow of the police station cells, albeit temporarily. Gavin appeared totally taken aback to see them.

"Sit down, Mr.Brooks," ordered D.I. Rogerson, then added without preamble, "there is something you are not telling us and I want to know what it is, no nonsense, no lies and no evasions, please."

Brooks shook his head as if in complete surprise as well as denial. He firmly denied that he had any more information to give. He had paid to men to kidnap his wife for ransom money, there was no more to be said.

In desperation, Rogerson decided on subterfuge, although he knew it could get him into serious trouble, later.

"Why is your wife packing her bags and preparing to leave. I understand her father is in Florida. Is she joining him? He had not heard so, when we contacted him. Why is Libby not staying to support you, Gavin?"

Gavin, however, remained silent. Then it came to Rogerson at last what had been niggling at his memory during the night.

"Why was your wife smiling after you had said your good-byes, yesterday, Gavin. I know you caught it as she was turning to go. Fleeting though it was, I saw something flash across your face. Was it surprise, or uncertainty? Tell us now and we may be able to help."

For a moment, all three thought that the prisoner was going to confide to them. Gavin appeared to be upset and put his head in his hands, but then he straightened up and asked for the guard to return him to his cell.

Nevertheless, all three detectives had been aware of a subtle change that had come over the prisoner. Back in the car, it was no surprise to his subordinates, when Rogerson ordered his sergeant to drive straight to Oak Tree Lane.

Once there, all three raced up to the top floor apartment. They rang the bell three times in quick succession and the door was straightaway opened by a welcoming Libby Brooks. But, seeing her face drop, they were aware the welcome was not intended for them.

"Why, whatever...?" She began, but the inspector interrupted her, brusquely as he pushed past her into the room beyond.

After they were all seated, he barked at her sternly.

"Well, you see, Mrs. Brooks, we are wondering why you are prepared to let your husband be charged alone with a serious crime, whilst you and your other partner, unbeknown to your husband, go free?"

Libby Brooks opened her mouth to speak, but again the inspector stopped her.

"No lies, please, Mrs. Brooks, we know you were in on the plan. What we don't know is why you smiled after seeing your husband being detained. Surely, that was upsetting and don't say I imagined it. I know what I saw. What is more, we have just come from visiting your husband and believe that he caught that strange reaction, too."

Libby Brooks began to splutter. "This is ridiculous, inspector. I am saying nothing more until I speak with my solicitor."

Before she could move, a key scraped in the lock of the door and a cheerful, familiar voice called out, "Hi, darling. We may not have the money, but I still have you!" The voice tailed off, as into the room bounded none other than young 'dimples' himself. As Mick gazed at them open mouthed, to the detectives' amazement, he was followed by an equally jubilant Julie!

'This will take some unraveling,' thought the D.I. taking note of the dismayed reaction of his young assistant.

Although taken aback at seeing who the newcomers were, he kept his expression stern. "Come in, Mr. and Mrs. Watkins, if indeed that is who you are. Do sit down and tell us all. By the way, you both look much smarter than when I last saw you. Now, I expect there have been several charades going on here. Enlighten us, please."

Mick and Julie sat on a sofa, looking as if their knees were buckling beneath them and then there was silence. More silence, accompanied by the three suspects sneaking questioning glances at one another. After some ten minutes or more had passed and it had become obvious that the police were not backing down, the room became noisy. There were angry indignant denials, followed by threats and aggressive gestures, but it became obvious, that the police were giving the impression that all was already known to them and they were not prepared to give an inch.

Finally, all the spluttering and shaking of heads came to a resigned stop. After a little persuasion that confession might lead to lighter sentences, the truth came tumbling out of Libby.

Mick was her lover and they wanted to be together. Julie was his sister and she had agreed to help them. They planned to put the blame on Gavin, who although he was involved, had no idea that Mark was Libby's partner in crime. Once he was in prison, Libby and Mark would be free to live together.

As if reading the inspector's mind, Libby explained that she would have ensured that she would be named as the potential victim and that Gavin would be blamed, whether or not the plan was successful. Then, even without ransom money, she was banking on her father feeling sorry for her being left 'alone'. She was sure he would have given her money. She had planned to ask him if she could stay in one of his luxurious places abroad. Then Mick would have joined her and Julie could have lived nearby, brother and sister being so close.

"Hmm," mused Rogerson. So they had a plan B for if both attempts had failed and there was no ransom money. Still, something didn't add up. Julie's part in this sunshine, sea and luxurious surroundings didn't quite fit. He made a swift decision and took a chance.

"I see that you had a plan B, Mrs. Brooks, but I am

afraid there was also a plan C. In a word or two, I think you have been had, as they say in the criminal world."

Libby stared at him with a puzzled frown as he continued.

"I suspect that we shall find that Mick and Julie are more than brother and sister after all. My dear, you were to be dumped, just as you betrayed your husband. Who needs money when there is an heiress to be blackmailed. One thing is certain, a father will pay any money to stop his daughter from going to jail, would he not?"

The inspector did not give the trio any time to react but had time to register the fury of the Watkins pair and the questioning bewilderment on the face of Libby Brooks, before they were all handcuffed and led away.

THE BICYCLE

The bicycle was leaning against the shed, its mudguard and tyres caked in brown and grey clay. The significance of the dirty tyres did not register. I viewed them unseeingly through the murkiness of my sluggish, early morning stupor.

The night had been long and restless and I had been caught and tossed about in a whirlwind of tiny fleeting images that threshed together to become one, long, terrifying nightmare. I had awakened with my mind still disturbed. I felt sick and frightened, my body shaking as my heart pounded deep inside me. I was afraid I would burst. Yet I could not remember what the nightmare had been about. I didn't try too hard. I preferred to leave it behind in the blank sleep that had at last come to me.

It was later that morning, that seeing the bicycle still there, I was stirred at least partly out of my stupor. Why should it be covered in mud? True, I had used it yesterday, just as I did every weekday, riding down to the village for my morning paper and a friendly chat with Old Parry at the store. The road to the village was long, but well-constructed, despite its narrowness. Farmers often drove their machines along it without mishap. It was certainly not usually covered in mud.

A sudden, unpleasant explanation came to me. Someone must have used the bicycle during the night. The thought of a stranger prowling around my garden brought an involuntary shudder. It was some time before my reasoning took me any further. If someone had taken it, for what reason and why had it been brought back? These questions pierced my still befuddled thoughts but brought no answers, only yet another question. Who could this mystery person be?

My thoughts began to clear a little. I thought back to the previous evening. Standing in the garden in the early morning sun, the stirrings of the unease I had felt last evening, came back to disturb me. Indeed, as I gazed at the bicycle, I fancied I could see an evil aural mist rising up, seeping from beneath the shed. I shook my head and when I looked again, the mist had gone.

I dropped down on my knees on the nearby path and busied myself frantically with the weeds thrusting up around the polyanthus plants. Gradually, my tugging became more controlled and as my bony knees began to protest at their labour, I stood up and sat on the bench by the porch. Calmer now, I was able to make a determined effort to trace back the events of the evening in some sort of order, so that I could follow my thoughts through, logically.

The knockings. It had been the knockings that had alarmed me. The first one had come at around seven o'clock. I remember I was dozing in the armchair before the fire.

However, by the time I had roused myself enough

to answer the door, my unknown visitor had gone. I am always slow moving these days, at least until I get going. My old enemy, Rheumatism, seems to be getting a hold on me. If it were not for the daily cycling, I think my knees would have seized up altogether, long before this. I have learnt to ignore the pain and carry on. Fight when threatened – that is my motto.

My thoughts returned to my musing. It was around eight, when I was just casting off the sleeve for Billy's new sweater, when the second knocking came, more insistent than before. I had jumped up as quickly as I could, dropping the knitting on the floor in my haste to reach the door. But again no visitor stood to greet me. The memory of the deserted door step now prompted me to leave the bench and begin weeding again. I dug my small fork in to the earth more fiercely as I recalled hurrying down the path to the gate and scanning the lane. But there had been no one in sight despite the evening being young and still reasonably light.

I stabbed at the same piece of earth over and over again, as I saw myself scurrying back inside the house and bolting all the doors and windows too. Secure though the house had become, I had been unable to resume my usual quiet evening pleasures. They had become forfeit to my fear. Instead, every sound had drawn my uneasy attention. The house was old and breathed naturally in creaks and small raps. Birds in the eaves? Mice in the skirtings? Leaves blowing gently on their twigs to tap against the porch window? Whereas all these sounds were familiar to me, last night they too had been suspect to me and were no longer easily identifiable.

The knockings had disturbed me more than I could have imagined. One moment I would chide myself for being a fanciful old woman, the next I sat and quivered in my chair. By the time I had summoned the courage to go upstairs to bed, my whole being had given itself up to nerves. Would the knockers return? Was someone intending to break in? What then? I had to pull the blankets well over my head, before eventually falling into those disquieting snatches of sleep. I was like a cowardly old ostrich.

Gradually, the regular action of the weeding, together with the clear morning air, restored me to something of my former self. The menace drifted away and the sun lit up the garden so that its colours came alive and smiled my blues further away. I came to a decision. I would go indoors, make myself a cup of tea, and then go down to the village to Mrs. McKnee's and find my Billy. The peace offering sweater was not finished but I would go anyway.

I cheered up as I thought about what I would say. I would tell him that I fully understood that he would want to get wed one day – and if the McKnee girl was what he wanted, well alright. But when he heard about the knockings, he would come home again, wouldn't he? He would want to be with me, protect me, for us to be together, just the two of us as we had always been, until he had met that young trollop. Once he was home again with his slippers warming before the fire and his favourite rhubarb tart in the oven, he would want to stay with his old ma. He would realise he belongs with me. Like I always told him and he was always happy about, until Ellie McKnee had come flashing her wild eyes at him.

I am enjoying my cup of tea now. Its hot sweetness is helping my returning feeling of well-being. I'll go and put my hat and coat on. Knocking. The knocking is coming back! The trembling has returned. Weak and with fumbling fingers, I open the door. Relief floods through me. This time, there is someone there. It's the Edwards boy, Constable Edwards as he is now, of course. How the years pass by. It seems only yesterday that he and Billy had used to spend many hours happily fishing for tiddlers in the brook. Give a boy a jam jar and a net, and he was a king. Now here was Clayton, standing before me at least six feet tall, in his uniform.

He is talking now, his rich, earthy voice subdued and as quiet as he could make it.

"Sit down, Mrs. Lewis, love." He spoke comfortingly and something jolts inside me. It starts up the motor within me and this in turn, joins with the pounding of my heart. The knocking is back, but this time it is louder than ever. He takes my arm and leads me to the armchair in such a gentle and considerate way. His large frame towers over me and he goes on speaking, but his words are drowned in the noise and turmoil inside my head.

It does not matter. I do not need to hear. I know what he is telling me, for I remember now – Billy and that girl lying together in the old bluebell dell, a mile or so up in the woods stretching away from the cottage. I remember particularly the stone, covered with her long black hair sticking to the blood that ran across it, trickling heavily into the grass. With satisfaction, I think now that Billy had hardly bled at all.

Clayton busies himself making me yet another cup of tea and stammers out a few disjointed words meant to console me. I glance down at the hem of my coat and see the brown and grey smudges of clay there.

First thing I must do when the Edwards boy leaves – is to clean my bicycle!

WHERE IS MRS BENT?

Mabs Graham lifted her thin rather gnarled hand and delicately moved aside a corner of the lace curtain, Keeping her face away from the window as much as possible, she gazed through her rheumy eyes out at the house opposite. It was about time. She did not have to wait long. The stout mock Tudor door opened and a man hurried out to his car in the drive. Slimly built and not too tall, he slid into the driving seat easily and drove off.

Mabs settled down for what had become her daily watch on the house. Beside her armchair, on a small table stood her tea-maker and a sandwich, although it was barely ten o'clock. She would leave the chair only when absolutely necessary, or when Mrs. Biggs or Alice were around to take over. She had had but little difficulty in convincing Mrs. Biggs that something very strange was happening across the road. The house was ordinary enough, small, detached, and with all the mock trimmings which allowed it to imitate the more graceful buildings of a past decade. Along the road, glass doors had been replaced with wooden doors reminiscent of the earlier days, and here and there bulbous curved bays with large bubbles in their glass, continued the pretence of age.

Alice was not so easy. Ten years younger than her sister Mabs, she was an active woman, lean and stringy and plain. She liked to be busy, and was not inquisitive by nature. Just now, she was mowing their small back lawn. She preferred to do the gardening in the morning, when their next door neighbour was out at work at the hospital. She found small talk over the fence irritating, and whilst not being unfriendly, did not make friends easily. If the truth were known, she was more interested in things than in people. She liked everything to be orderly. Inside the house, she could lay her hand on any tool or utensil or item of household equipment immediately. Everything had its own place and now that Mabs was too fragile to do much around the house, in its place it stayed.

Mabs wished Mrs. Biggs would hurry up and come so that she could give her eyes a rest. Three days of peering out at the house opposite were beginning to tell. Her eyes tended to blur and they felt sore and tired. As in the past days, there was no sign of movement in the house.

"He's done her in," she whispered to herself for the umpteenth time, her choice of words showing the influence of television on someone who had always in her younger days been genteel in dress and speech.

Mrs. Biggs popped her head around the door briskly. She was large and florid but moved with a swift ease her bulk belied.

"Shan't be above half an hour, Mrs. G. Is there anything you want before I pop upstairs?"

"Just come here and take over for a few minutes to give my poor eyes a rest," replied Mabs in her breathless voice, but her words held no self-pity and her eyes were gleaming behind the glasses with something akin to excitement.

"Right you are, Mrs. G.," smiled Mrs. Biggs good-naturedly. She cast a backward glance first to make sure that Alice was still busily pre-occupied in the garden, then crossed the room to where a small glass ash-tray now held the slightly askew curtain in place. She stood beside the old lady's chair and peered steadily out. At first she had been humouring the old lady, but now she was beginning to admit to herself that the old dear might not be losing her marbles after all. There was something decidedly odd about Mr. Brent. She had been in the corner shop near her daughter's house a mile or two away when he had popped in for some cigarettes yesterday. She couldn't define it, but there was something weird about him. He had gone before she had a chance to study him further. Apart from his appearance she had been surprised to see him over in Carndon. The area was largely a huddle of run-down streets packed too close together. Surely he did not work over there? There were only one or two small foundries and small back street one man factories and repair garages in the area and she did not need to be told he was not the type to get his hands dirty. Too – she struggled for the word – too effeminate by half.

"Squat on the arm of my chair, Mrs. Biggs," Mabs urged. She had heard all about Mrs. Biggs meeting him in the shop but she had some news of her own.

"Oh you two are not at it again," her sister's voice came from the door in a grumble but belied by a tolerant grin. "You're keeping Mrs. Biggs from her work again, Mabs."

"I'm just relieving her for a few minutes, Miss Eames," said Mrs. Biggs apologetically, managing to convey that she was there purely for Mrs. Graham's sake.

Alice snorted, "I don't know why you encourage her. Well I only came through to see if you were alright, Mabs, so I'll get back to the garden."

"Perhaps that's what he is doing at nights," suggested Mabs allowing herself an expressive shudder, "digging his garden."

"You've been reading too many books, and watching too much television," Alice laughed, and promptly disappeared.

Mabs turned to Mrs. Biggs eagerly.

"Keep your eyes open, Mrs Biggs," she warned as the daily turned her face towards her. "There was a man there this morning, knocking on the door as if he were going to break it down. I was paying the milkman as slowly as I could, I can tell you Mrs. Biggs. Well after banging on the front door, he went around the side and tried the gate, but it was locked. Then he came back and peered through the windows. Then the milkman spoiled everything by calling across to him and asking if he could help. The man shook his head and mumbled something and drove off in a very flashy car, very flashy." She nearly added, "like gangsters use on television," but thought perhaps Mrs. Biggs would think she was being too fanciful. She did not want Mrs. Biggs to scoff at her like Alice. She needed an ally when things began to happen as she was sure they soon would.

Mabs need not have worried. Mrs. Biggs was way ahead of her.

"He had a contract out on her," she was thinking. She was frowning with concentration, but inside she was excited. She was enjoying every moment of whatever drama she or Mrs. Graham could make out of it.

"Go on, Mrs. G.," she urged, her eyes still peering across the road.

"Well, no one had answered obviously, but after the man had gone, I saw the curtain draw back a little and just for a moment a face at the window."

"She's still alive," breathed Mrs. Biggs in awe, and with a keen sense of disappointment. "Well, well that's a turn up for the books."

"Ah, I think not, Mrs. Biggs," declared Mabs dramatically. She was coming to the best part now. "It was a woman, but it was definitely not Mrs. Brent. Now then, what do you think of that, Mrs. Biggs?"

Mrs. Biggs thought a lot of it. Her large frame trembled with excitement.

"How do you know that, Mrs. G.?" she asked in awe, but total belief.

"Because it was a redhead, that's how," answered Mabs with an air of triumph, "and what's more she was dressed in something very bright and shiny, a most horrible bright green, it was, not nice Mrs. Brent's style at all."

Mrs. Biggs was dubious. She rather liked bright colours herself.

"Lots of people wear gaudy nightwear what wouldn't walk the streets in the same colours," she protested, "and she could have dyed her hair. Perhaps —" she added as if light had suddenly dawned, "— perhaps that's why she didn't turn up for coffee last Friday. She'd dyed her hair and thought you might not approve. Or perhaps she made a mess of it. Young people set a lot of store on how they look, don't forget, and she'd he embarrassed for you to see it I shouldn't wonder. Yes, that's all it was after all." She didn't know whether to be disappointed that Mrs. Brent was still alive or happy that she could now go on with the upstairs in peace. Her neck was beginning to ache from being in one place for so long.

"No. It wasn't her, I'm certain," Mabs insisted. "Even from that distance I could see she was plastered in make-up, I mean her cheeks could have been red from sleeping, but her lips were bright orange. I would have had to be blind not to see that, and dumb to think it would be Mrs. Brent. She's always so delicately made up, you know?"

"Well, Mrs. G., I'll have to get on upstairs or Miss Evans will be breathing down my neck and rightly so. Call me the moment you see anything unusual," she added as a sop, "and I'll keep a look out now and then from upstairs." She manoeuvred her bulk around the armchair and went out swiftly before Mrs. Graham could detain her any longer.

A visitor thwarted any further attempts of

surveillance, so Mabs resigned herself to waiting until evening to see if anything transpired. She chatted with her visitor attentively and pleased her sister by making no reference to the house opposite or to the Brents. Upstairs Mrs. Biggs worked methodically with her usual thoroughness, allowing herself a fleeting glance out of the front bedroom window when cleaning that room, and conveniently using the same window from which to shake her duster when working elsewhere.

The evening was a disappointment. Mr. Brent returned home long after Mabs and Alice had retired, for once unseen by Mabs who had retired early, feeling very fatigued. She also had a stiff shoulder which made it awkward for her to undress, but she refrained from asking Alice to rub her shoulder with a heat ointment. She knew she would get a well-deserved lecture.

Alice slept well after her strenuous gardening, but Mabs tossed and turned, succumbing only to light dozing. Once as car lights swept around the bedroom, she sat up in bed and strained to see across the road, but the house was dark and its occupants seemingly asleep. She longed to get out of bed to sit at the window, since she couldn't sleep anyway, but she knew that that would really make Alice cross, and think her obsessed.

The thought that she could be making a fool of herself did cross her mind. Perhaps she was just a silly old woman with too much time on her hands. However, deep down she was certain she had genuine grounds for suspicion. Mrs. Brent had been in the habit of popping over for coffee once a week for almost three months.

On the two occasions before that she had not arrived, she had either phoned or dropped in an apologetic note through the door. Both times she had had a migraine, and both times she had appeared the next morning and invited herself for coffee then, instead. Mabs guessed she was lonely. The Brents had moved into the road barely a year ago and Mabs seemed to be one of the few people with whom any contact had been made. Most of the neighbours were out at work during the day. Indeed it was unusual these days for a young wife without children not to be at work. Mr. Brent rarely brought anyone home from work, and indeed had given up his Civil Service post for what Mrs. Brent had vaguely termed as something which involved having to see clients in the evening. Alice had decided he was in insurance, but since Mrs. Brent's non-appearance for coffee and her husband's weak excuse that she had been called away suddenly, Mabs had been thinking hard. One thing was for sure, insurance talks did not go on till past midnight every night. Nor did wives who had gone off to look after sick relatives, open the door to the postman next morning.

It was since Mabs had seen the latter incident that she had begun to feel uneasy. She had waved across to Mrs. Brent expecting her to slip across and explain why she had not in fact gone away after all, since that was the reason her husband had given only the day before, but Mrs. Brent had shut the door hurriedly. Mabs still could not explain why she had begun to watch the house that very morning, but watch it she had for the past three days and not once had she seen a sign of Mrs. Brent. Lying there in the dark room, she thought back to list the incidents that had alerted her imagination, as if to justify her actions to herself. The obviously invented excuse for not coming over for coffee, the failure of Mrs. Brent to follow up her absence with any other explanation or visit, the man knocking on the door so persistently, the redhead at the window, Mr. Brent's appearance in a very seedy district looking odd as Mrs. Biggs had described more colourfully, and his arrival home in the small hours. If his wife had been ill, surely he would have popped back to see her. Lastly, something which Mabs had not dared tell Alice, Mabs herself had slipped over the road and rung the bell, calling through the letter box to ask if she were alright. No one had answered, yet she knew Mrs. Brent had not gone out, since even when she had left the room for the bathroom, either Mrs. Biggs or Alice had been cajoled to keep an eye on the house for her.

When she finally dropped off to sleep, she had a weird dream of her sister digging graves in the garden and negotiating a price with Mr. Brent for him to have one. She awoke late, flustered and feeling as tired as if she had not slept at all. Glancing at the clock she was dismayed to see it was almost eleven. She dressed quickly although her fingers were losing their grip these days and buttons had become a nuisance to her.

Downstairs to her surprise, she found Alice in her place at the window. Her sister turned defensively and explained.

"I thought I'd never hear the end of it if I didn't keep tabs for you," she said. "I could see you were fast asleep, so I thought you should have a lie-in. All this excitement can't be good for your blood pressure."

"There's nothing wrong with my blood pressure. I've got poor circulation, that's all. But, Alice, it was good of you to keep watch for me. Does that mean I've managed to convince you at last?"

"No," said Alice firmly. "It means I didn't want to see your long face for the rest of the day if you thought you had missed something." She went out to make a pot of tea and some toast for her sister. Opposites they might be, but they were exceedingly fond of each other, and Alice was grateful to Mabs for offering her a home.

An hour later, Mabs called her sister excitedly. Alice dropped the potato knife into the bowl of water and rushed into the living room. Mabs was pointing across at the house opposite, and joining her at the window as discreetly as possible, she watched as Mr. Brent could be seen lifting what appeared to be a substantial bundle of lady's clothing into the back seat of his car. The two sisters remained silent as he drove hurriedly away. Whatever was happening there was something Alice could not deny. His manner had been decidedly furtive.

"Before I called you, Bill Owen came out of the house next door and Mr. Brent dived back into the house as fast as he could. Then he reappeared as soon as Bill's car had gone up towards town. Come on, Alice, admit I may be right after all."

Alice was too down to earth to be so easily swayed,

but she did concede something peculiar seemed to be going on.

"Not a murder though Mabs, I won't go along with that. If you want to know what I think, I think she's left him and he is avoiding the neighbours because he doesn't want to talk about it."

"Well I'm sorry, but I think it's time I did something," said Mabs, crossing the room and lifting the telephone.

"What are you doing, girl? You're not calling the police?" cried Alice moving across to stop her. "Don't be foolish, Mabs, you'll make yourself a laughing stock."

"I'm not ringing the police and yet I am," answered Mabs provocatively. Seeing her sister's exasperated puzzlement, she paused teasingly before enlightening her. "I'm going to ask Jane to pop over. I'll just tell her the facts and see if she thinks I ought to report it or not. Now you can't quarrel with that can you?"

Alice could not. Jane was their niece. Capable, hard-working and practical she had joined the Police Service after two years of tedious work at a newspaper office, and had risen quickly up to the rank of Sergeant. Alice was sure that Jane would make conciliatory comments to her beloved Aunt Mabs and then let the matter drop.

In part Alice was right. When Jane arrived at five o'clock just between shifts, she listened to her aunt and made her list all her reasons in an orderly fashion, which was not easy when Mabs was excited for her words tumbled out in jumps and jerks of memory. Eventually however Jane was in the picture and to Alice's dismay the conciliatory remarks did not come over as an attempt to appease. She had not made allowances for the two years Jane had spent working for a newspaper. Jane had learnt to follow up any lead however unpromising they had seemed at first, so now, though her common sense told her the facts hardly added up to likely criminal activity, her flair for news instinctively urged her to follow this one up. She left her aunts with a promise to look into it and to be in touch, leaving one aunt ecstatic and the other envisaging a suit for slander.

Mabs had been persuaded by Alice to refrain from her daylong surveillances, now that Jane was going to make discreet inquiries for them.

"You'll get stiff, dear, and then your circulation troubles will start all over again. At our age it is important to keep active. Come and do a little hoeing, that won't hurt you and it will do you more good than sitting down all day, and in one spot too," she added, "craning your very inquisitive neck." So Mabs contented herself with an occasional peek through the curtains. After tea however, she thought she had earned a little snoop, and settled down in her usual chair. She was soon rewarded.

Mr. Brent's car was in the drive and occasionally she caught glimpses of him. Then she caught her breath, for standing in the kitchen window, was a redhead, undoubtedly female and much taller than 'poor Mrs. Brent'. She wore an apron and appeared to be washing up. Mabs wondered if she should slip over on some pretext or other. There would be no harm in making friendly enquiries as to when Mrs. Brent was likely to return, but she decided against it. Alice would disapprove and perhaps Jane wouldn't like it either now that they had consulted her. So she contented herself with unashamed peeking. A little later, she saw the redhead through the living room window of the house opposite. She seemed to be walking back and forth almost as if practising to be a model, Mabs thought smiling at her own imaginative fancies. At a quarter to seven the redhead fleetingly passed an upstairs window.

"Well," breathed Mabs, scandalised again. "She's up there again, Alice," she said breathlessly. "I don't know what to make of it I'm sure." Despite her excitement, she soon began to have a little doze, waking just in time to see Mr. Brent's car leaving. He appeared to be on his own. The time was 7.30 p.m.

Alice refused to allow Mabs to stay up late enough to catch his homecoming. She turned Mabs' chair determinedly round and negotiated her into a game of Scrabble. Normally Mabs revelled in the game, but this evening her concentration was weak and neither lady finished a game with a creditable score.

Next morning, a telephone call from Jane put Mabs into a fluster.

"Auntie, Mrs. Brent is home. She will pop over to see you at about seven this evening, if that's alright with you?"

For a moment Mabs was speechless.

"Well, really?" she asked after a slight pause. "I mean, well, that will be nice, dear, but couldn't she come over for coffee this morning instead. I mean," she went on, stammering a little over her words, "shouldn't she be at home for Mr. Brent then?"

Jane's reply left her even more non-plussed.

"Oh, he'll be along too, aunty. Can't say more now, I've got to dash. My love to Aunt Alice," and Mabs was left holding the receiver.

"Whatever is the matter, Mrs. G.?" asked Mrs. Biggs, her round face florid from her efforts in the kitchen, and looking rather concerned.

When Mabs told her, she felt equally bemused.

"There, all our theories gone down the drain with one telephone call," she laughed. "Come on, I'll pour you a nice glass of Madeira, you've had a nasty shock," and she laughed again.

"Thanks, Mrs. Biggs. Pour one for yourself too." replied Mabs weakly. She felt a little foolish, especially at having to face Alice with this latest development, but when her sister came in later, there was no "I told you so." Surprisingly, she looked sceptical.

"Wait until the day is over. We may yet have another written excuse when seven o'clock comes."

They did not have a written excuse, but a shock, the first of a trio of shocks in fact. When the doorbell rang promptly at seven, who should be standing at the door, but a very theatrical looking red-head.

"May I come in, Mrs. Graham?" she asked softly, her voice belying her flamboyant dress of bright vermillion, and the gaudy orange boa flung carelessly around her shoulders. Mabs would have shook her head if she had not caught sight of Jane behind. As it was, Jane, had to edge herself and the red-head through the doorway.

"You'd better sit down, Aunt Mabs," she smiled.

Mabs was too bemused to be very observant but as soon as they entered the living room, Alice saw that her niece was enjoying herself hugely, and as she showed them graciously to the settee, she could not help considering that the joke was probably on them.

Mabs soon found her voice.

"I don't understand," she said icily. "I understood Mrs. Brent was coming."

"And come I have," said the voice of the red-head, this time sounding just like young Mrs. Brent.

"Just sit still and watch, Aunty," advised Jane, a smile still persisting at the corners of her mouth.

Mabs was not too overcome, when the red-head swiftly removed her red curls to reveal the short blonde tresses of Mrs. Brent. She was coming round to the idea that their nice young friend might have taken to dressing herself up in this most distasteful way, for some reason. She watched as the woman opposite her deftly delved into a vanity case and brought out a bottle of cleanser and a wad of cotton wool. Dabbing the wool with some of the oil, Mrs. Brent began to remove the heavy tan make-up, carefully avoiding the skin around the overly made-up eyes.

"I wonder if you ladies would mind turning your faces away from me just for a moment?" she asked. Both women complied tactfully, assuming the vermillion was next to be removed, whilst Jane continued to look on.

"You can turn back now," the familiar soft voice told them. To their surprise they saw that not only had the dress been replaced by a white silk shirt and cord trousers, but the thick eyelashes had also gone. Before them was the quietly dressed, familiar face of their young neighbour.

"Now will you tell us why you have been dressing up so so weirdly," Mabs struggled for the right words, hoping she was not being too offensive. "What a let down all this is for Poor Mrs. Biggs," she thought, her own disappointment all too keen.

"I haven't quite finished, but I'll use the bathroom if you don't mind," smiled Mrs. Brent. Alice stood up to show her the way with an accommodating smile. Puzzled, she sensed a further surprise imminent, but Jane remained adamantly tightlipped.

Surprise it certainly was, when some time later, into the room, the blonde hair replaced by short dark waves, and a tie at the neck. There nervously confronting them, was not the expected Mrs. Brent, but her husband.

Alice was the first to recover.

"There is no Mrs. Brent," she gasped. "It was you all the time!"

"Good, you've guessed. That makes explanations a little easier. All the same, I will leave those to Jane, if you don't mind." He looked across at Jane both hopefully and apprehensively, and sank down into an armchair.

"John is a drag artist, Aunty. He 'does' the halls pretty well all around the district. When Sgt. Wilkinson went round to make tentative enquiries for me, he recognised him straight away."

John took up the story.

"You see, I really want to go around the world, see

life whilst I am still without ties. I've been planning the trip for a long time, but when I was made redundant last September, all seemed hopeless. Then one of my mates began telling me about his cousin who was making a good income for himself as a drag artist. Well we'd had a few drinks and for a laugh we went to see him perform, over at Churchbridge. I must have been drunk or I would never have got interested, but next day he was on my doorstep. Apparently I had asked for advice, and well — I decided to have a go when he showed me the thickest wad of notes I've seen in my lifetime, and I thought, 'Hawaii, here I come.'"

John paused but did not look directly at the ladies as if afraid to read downright disapproval in their eyes. He went on.

"Mum and dad bought the house over the road and I agreed to live there and look after it until Dad retires next month. So I thought, I'd practise on my neighbours. If they took me for a woman then I felt I would have the confidence to go on stage. It's much harder to pass as an ordinary woman in daylight you know. When you accepted me, I felt really good and signed a contract directly afterwards. I wanted to tell you I was a man when you were so kind to me. I hated deceiving you, honestly. That's why I thought it best to stop coming round. Please forgive me."

Mabs and Alice were speechless. Mabs felt robbed of her 'murder,' but her sense of humour came quickly to the fore and she smiled across at him, shaking her head waggishly.

Meanwhile the practical Alice said, "I think we could all do with a nice cup of tea," and went off into the kitchen. She too was smiling and once inside the kitchen allowed herself an embarrassed little giggle. "What a world we live in," she thought. "Who would have thought we should ever entertain a drag artist."

Later, as they said good-bye, they urged him to continue his coffee visits.

"Bring the blonde or the redhead too," grinned Jane as their relieved visitor took his leave.

Mabs and Alice passed the evening in somewhat hysterical mood, chuckling to themselves at intervals and giggling whenever their eyes met. As she prepared for bed that night, Mabs suddenly wondered if any of Mr. Brent's disguises or mannerisms when on stage, were modelled on her or Alice. Mentally, she avowed to have her hair done in a new style.

SISTERS

J essie had known for years that both her sisters hated
her. She knew that Joanne, the youngest of the three
still blamed her for sending away her one and only suitor.
She had never been able to forgive despite the passing
years and made no attempt to disguise her loathing. Poor
Joanne. She had always been plain, her face narrow and
pinched, its skin sallow and her small eyes just slightly
too close together. Nowadays, those eyes were blank.
The only gleam of life came when she had to come face
to face with Jessie, a gleam of pure malice.

As she sat in the old rocker that had been their
mother's favourite chair, Jessie thought back to the days
when John Templeton had entered their narrow lives.
Their days had been an endless repetition of serving in
their parents' Draper's shop, Jessie doing the accounts
in the evenings and her younger sisters sharing the
domestic duties, not to mention the nursing of first
their father and then their querulous ailing mother.
Jessie had found the suave young gentleman too suave
by half and seeing him encouraging the simpering
Joanne in her adoration made her both greatly irritated
and contemptuous. As for Mary-Anne, her other
sister, she paused in her thoughts for a moment as she

attempted to gather them together, but she could find no reason to them.

It was strange but true that she had no real idea why Mary-Anne should feel so venomously antagonistic towards her, nor could she recall when such unexpected animosity had come to her notice. She knew only that it had grown and mushroomed from a vague inkling that all was not well, at such an alarming speed that the Edwardian walls of the house seemed to breathe in and out, malice and indeed a suppressed violence. Now that the shop was closed and they were thrown into each other's more leisurely company, Jessie knew without doubt that Mary-Anne could scarcely bear to be in the same room with her, pushing Joanne's antipathy into the background where it lurked quietly in the shadows of the musty old house.

The minutes ticked by on the old Grandfather clock in the corner and a sly smile slithered momentarily across Jessie's pale face. It had gone as quickly as it had come. The hatred, never voiced, never openly acknowledged, did not frighten her. Despite being old now and fairly infirm, the menace did not affect her in the expected way. Instead, she hugged it into herself, allowing excitement to course through her thin blood. She had always been the strong one, some would say cold and unfeeling. Now she felt the aversion towards her stimulating. It gave interest to the long days. It was something to think about as time dragged her on into a tedious, inactive old age. Now she sat still in the stiff-backed horsehair chair, her equally stiff corsets keeping her back upright as ever. She was unaware of the dim, musty parlour. Its heavy drapes kept outside any intrusive rays of sunlight that modern people seemed to let into their houses these days, alongside, of all things, so called 'fresh' air. Undisturbed with her book sat open but unattended on her lap, she deliberated as she had done so many times before, a slight glint in the eyes somehow giving her gaunt face a malicious gleam.

"Now, when did I first become aware of the change in Mary-Anne?" she mused. We got on so well as children, even Joanne, although her constant whining didn't make her the most endearing child. There had been some ill-feeling later, when as the eldest sister, she was given the more interesting post of keeper of the accounts, but that had quickly passed, she was sure.

Jessie struggled to fight off drowsiness as the heat from the coals added to the stifling stuffiness of the room. She always seemed to nod off before her thoughts could really take off. Feebly she reached for her stick and levered herself awkwardly out of the chair. She made her way slowly across the faded carpet and sank down onto the window seat. She could feel no air coming in, no draught of which her mother had so habitually complained, but it was well away from the blazing fire and cooler. She did not want to go to sleep today. She wanted to worry her way through the problem, once and for all. For some reason, it was important to her that the answer be found today. She rested her back against a hard but plump cushion and made herself concentrate.

Her mind drifted back into the past. Had not

Mary-Anne's coldness come about the time that John Templeton had suddenly disappeared out of a distraught Joanne's frigid life? It was puzzling and hard to remember because at that time her attention had been focussed on Joanne. Surely though, Mary-Anne had supported Jessie in her disapproval of Joanne's infatuation? She had even offered to take over their youngest sister's sick-visiting duties in the Parish, a practice continued long after their father had ceased to be regarded by the villagers as a main benefactor. Old habits die hard together with a sense of heritage and duty. With John giving Joanne the cold shoulder, admittedly shocking in its suddenness, Mary-Anne had visited the sick regularly and uncomplainingly, whilst poor Joanne sobbed hysterically in her bedroom for hours on end, blaming Jessie for sending him away. Jessie had never defended herself. She was unable to get through her sister's grief to get her attention and it was unlikely that she would be believed. Instead, she had undertaken all the considerable domestic duties of this claustrophobic old house.

As the room darkened even further into the late afternoon, Jessie nodded. Yes, Mary-Anne had been in total agreement with her. Joanne was much too young to be courting. She was barely into her twenties. Besides it was unthinkable that she should wed before her older sisters. She screwed up her eyes as if trying to peer right through the gloom of the room, into a not much brighter past.

Almost instantly a picture of Mary-Anne came to her, standing at the french windows of the withdrawing room, looking quite handsome despite her boney face. She was wearing her new green gown, and holding the basket of new-laid eggs covered over with a lace napkin, well away from her as if she were afraid to soil her dress. Jessie's thoughts took a jolt. Something bothered her about that dress, but the doubt escaped before she could address it. Instead, she continued her reverie, recalling Mary-Anne's rather self-righteous words.

"Don't fret, Jessie. You were duty bound to send that young man away. Joanne is not only young, but silly and immature for her age. Now, until she regains her senses and that includes her sense of responsibility to others less fortunate than herself, I shall undertake the administering to the sick. I shall continue in the way Father would have wished."

Jessie sighed, an old woman's quavering sigh, as the picture of the past faded. She struggled to bring it back. It wasn't so much the words, but something about that smug, smiling image of Mary-Anne disturbed her. What was it that should so disquieten her? As she sought to recapture that figure in green, her brow cleared. Of course! Mary-Anne had been about to go into the tiny steam and smoke-filled hovels of the miners wearing her new green gown! For heavens' sake, why would she even consider going near those cottages so dressed? The muddy rubbish laden lanes would have caused havoc with hems of dress and petticoats. Who would approach such filth in a best dress?

Jessie's reverie was abruptly interrupted as Mary-Anne entered the room. Her hair was no longer the shining crown of chestnut in the picture, but straggled and streaked with grey and fading brown. The green dress was very much a figment of the past. This afternoon, she wore an unattractive blue house frock, one of a succession of dull, ordinary frocks she habitually now wore. Mary-Anne took no notice of her sister, but removed the straw hat and old gloves she wore when tending the garden and crossed the room to place them upon the polished occasional table near the far wall, a gesture aimed solely to annoy her sister. But for once Jessie did not notice. Her strident voice cut icily across her sister's path, its unexpected strength bringing Mary-Anne to a startled halt.

"Why were you wearing your new green dress that day?"

That day had been over twenty years before but Jessie saw by the immediate stiffening of her sister's boney shoulders, that there was really no need to enlarge. However, she was not quite prepared for the look of pure hatred that flashed across the room to where she sat upright and expectant. Since her sister remained mute, Jessie persisted.

"You hate me too, more perhaps than Joanne does. Why? Oh don't think I mind," she added hastily. "I care neither one way or the other but I do think I am entitled to know the reason."

Mary-Anne's mouth twisted before she eventually spoke.

"Hate you?" the words came in thin strangled sounds. "Hate you? I despise you. You took away my only chance of happiness and con – condemned me to this dreary decaying house for the rest of my life. And now, you sit there and ask why?" Her voice faltered. She placed both rather gnarled hands on a chair and leaned hard, her head drooping in an attitude of despair.

Jessie viewed her sister calmly, a hint of cold pleasure in the curl of her thin lips. She did not understand but she had been right about one thing. It would be interesting. After the monotony of her life and not just of her declining years, her senses stirred into a forgotten eagerness.

"Perhaps you could control yourself long enough to offer me an explanation I can understand?" she remarked, showing a complete lack of sympathy for her sister's distress. Her reserve unleashed Mary-Anne's wavering loss of control. Raising her head, her words stormed across the stuffy parlour.

"You cold hearted slug," she hissed, her face contorted and red with anger. "Yes, slug. That is exactly what you are. You took away my John. It was you who sent him half across the world with no more than the briefest of goodbyes, and that not from his lips but scrawled hurriedly across a piece of notepaper. You might as well have taken my life." She paused, "Why didn't you. Oh dear God, why didn't you?" Jessie was too taken aback to comment on the blasphemy. She watched in amazement as her sister banged the table with her fists and then sank onto a chair, stifling sobs that somehow she managed to contain within the back of her throat. Indeed, she was more intrigued than ever.

"YOUR John? For heaven's sake, Mary-Anne, the years have addled your brains. You appear to be totally deranged. If he belonged to anyone, it was to Joanne, and I seem to remember that you were in complete agreement when I forbade him to visit for a while to see if his interest would continue after a separation. Am I not right?"

Mary-Anne lifted her head wearily, as if it had gained a tremendous weight.

"No, you are not right. You are quite, quite wrong. He was mine – mine, do you hear? Oh he was interested in Joanne at first it is true, but when I offered to take secret messages from Joanne to him, it was me he fell in love with. He soon realised that his feelings for her were nothing more than an immature passion, for an equally immature girl."

Mary-Anne paused for breath. Her face was alive now, red and glowing from memories of love before it was blown away. It was then that Jessie noticed the shadow of their youngest sister thrown by the flickering fire against the doorway. She was vastly amused but gave no sign. Instead, she fixed her gaze firmly on Mary-Anne's face and coldly awaited the next onslaught of words to come tumbling out of those trembling lips. This was not only interesting. This was fun!

"That afternoon, I was taking the eggs for the last time. John had promised to meet me at the old oak tree behind Mrs. Jones' cottage. Once I had taken old Will Jones' medicine for his bronchitis, we were going to go away together. Oh I was so impatient. The birds were singing along the lanes and I wished we could take off and fly as they could. The sun shone down and I was hot but I hurried on. I paid all my calls, I didn't miss one. I owed that to dear Papa and it seemed an age before I reached The Jones' cottage. To my dismay, Will had taken for the worse and Mrs. Jones was both distraught and helpless. There was nothing I could do but stay awhile. I placed a cool, moist cloth on the old man's forehead, as a fever took hold of him. I remember trying to hold him still as his body shook and all the time I was thinking soon I would be with John and I should never see the village or this house again. I even remember I felt sad that I should not see you and Joanne again. That should amuse you, shouldn't it?"

Mary Anne paused again and wiped her perspiring brow with a dainty handkerchief kept back from unsold stock. The shadow behind her was stronger now, but she was completely unaware of a third presence easing itself silently into the room, or of the sense of evil it portended. There was silence a moment as if she could not force out the words that had to come. Then the flow resumed.

"At last the doctor and Gwyn Jones arrived. I murmured a few words of comfort, then fled from them like a mad woman. When – when I reached the old oak, he wasn't there. For a moment I was stunned, then I ran around the tree, looking in all directions and I saw him. I saw him –" she faltered again and her voice was strange in its despair. She shook her head and the words began to pour out again.

"I saw him. He had crossed the fields and must have been a quarter of a mile away. I watched unbelievingly as he jumped up onto Evan Davies' old cart and went rumbling away, rumbling right out of my life. I waved and waved frantically, running across the fields as fast as a hare. Then he began to wave too, but not to me. He was waving to you Jessica, my precious sister. You were standing on the old stone wall of Evan Davies' farmhouse, happily waving him out of my life." She shuddered. "I can still feel the coldness that crept over and into my body that day."

Mary-Anne shuddered then went on.

"I turned towards the oak again, frantically searching for a message. At this stage I still hoped there was just a delay and he would soon return. There was a note of course, written by his hand. It was short and to the point, oh brutally to the point!"

Behind her, the shadow seemed to shudder into life but came no nearer. Jessie's eyes gleamed in anticipation.

"I'm intrigued Mary-Anne. Do tell me what was in the letter. How did this wonderful lover of yours explain his somewhat hurried departure?"

Mary-Anne told her, her voice becoming toneless with remembered shock.

"Forgive me," he had written. "Forgive me for not waiting to say goodbye, but say goodbye I must. Your sister has seen fit to inform me of the family difficulties that you, my dear, should have told me long since. I appreciate that with your family history of insanity, it was wise and proper for your father to direct in his will, that apart from sufficient sums being put aside to enable you and your sisters to live in reasonable comfort, the rest of his money should go to charities variously specified. But, money shortage aside, I cannot take the risk, dear Mary-Anne of any symptoms showing themselves in you. I should be watching daily for the signs of which your sister so graphically spoke. It is best I leave." Mary-Anne said no more, for in truth she had been unable to continue to read any further. The note had fluttered out of her trembling fingers, to be lifted on the breeze maybe to follow the cart on its journey.

Jessie's eyes swivelled towards the looming shadow moving reluctantly away to focus on her distraught sister.

"You're a fool, Mary-Anne! You always were. How could I have waved him off? Was I not in the kitchen making pounds of jam – damson, plum, greengages bubbling away on the range? How could I have possibly left the kitchen on such an errand? No, sister, It was not I waving to your precious John Templeton."

Mary-Anne looked at her in complete disbelief and then found herself held by the logic. Then she started as behind her a voice giggled.

"She's right, Mary-Anne. You are a fool." Mary-Anne's spine prickled. The menace held her and she dared not move her head. The voice hissed on, keeping her shocked into rigid stillness.

"Did you think I would let you have him? You thought you were so clever sneaking off to meet him. Do you think I would stay locked in my room with you out of the house and Jessie too busy to keep watch? I simply told him the truth. You were mad, mad to believe that I wouldn't sense your eagerness to take my messages, and madder to believe I would not sense the change of tone in John's replies. No. I would never let you have him. He was not worth having anyway. He had promised to love me forever, but he transferred his affections at the first hurdle."

The words were scarcely more than a whisper now and took on a new wheedling tone.

"I did it for your own good, Mary-Anne. Isn't it funny how you've hated Jessie all these years, when it should have been me? I can't tell you how much I have enjoyed watching you two together. It has been my only pleasure." The whispering chuckle dried up and for the first time Mary-Anne turned and she and her sister came face to face.

When Mary-Anne spoke, it was with her old calmness.

"You are quite correct," she said. "We will now forget the matter. If you will both excuse me, I will get tea." She left the room, her head erect, her pose normal. Joanne stood still a while, in shocked surprise, then meekly she followed.

On the window seat, Jessie no longer smiled. For so long the house had pulsated with mutual hatred. There had finally become something comforting about hate. It was exciting. It had gradually taken her out of the dull life of impoverished spinsterhood, to feed her daily with the suspense on which she had come to thrive.

Slowly the smile crept back into her watery eyes. After today, far from abating, the house would pulse with the hatred of all three, equal shares now. It would be intriguing to see what Mary-Anne might do. She was obviously in a state of numbness now, but the shock would wear off.

Of course, Jessie would have to see that nothing would be allowed to be forgotten, a little nudge here and there. She smiled more broadly than she had for a very long time. Life would never be dull again!

THE
CHRISTMAS CARD

"Cheerio, Mr Jones, see you on Boxing Day. Don't forget to open your card," and then the door slammed shut and his carer had gone, leaving William to face anther lonely day.

When he was young, Christmas had been such a happy time. Although presents were small and few, he had been surrounded by love and laughter. Now, musing in his old armchair, with a blanket over his knees, William Jones finished the soup his carer had made for him and within minutes had dozed off.

When he came to, he reached out for the Christmas card. Glancing at the others on the mantelpiece, he calculated this was card number four; two from carers, one from a neighbour and one from his old pal David.

"This is what Christmas had come to," he said to himself.

He opened the envelope with his shaking, stiff fingers and glanced at the picture. Then he struggled to his feet to place the card with the others. Carefully he put it on the end where the weak winter sun picked up its sparkle. Then he peered at it more closely.

There was something about the picture that made him pause. He picked it up again, puzzled, trying to remember the flash of recognition that had caught his attention.

Slowly, card in hand, he sat back into his chair and looked at it more closely. It was a cheerful scene. There was of a cluster of snow-capped village houses, with a large decorated Christmas tree sparkling beside the end house. To the fore was a brook, with people bearing presents crossing its bridge, and children with brightly coloured hats and scarves skating happily on its iced-over surface.

In his muddled old head, a memory was trying to surface. Then he focused on the lamp post, its bright light shining in through the bedroom window of the first house. He gasped. Of course! The cluster of houses, the brook and the light shining in through the bedroom window, were all so familiar. It could have been a picture of the very part of the village where he had grown-up and subsequently lived with his wife Edith.

The house on the end, was just where his house had been, overlooking the brook and the bridge. The children skating could have been his brothers and sisters, his oldest brother holding his hand.

Their house had not been so clean and picturesque looking, for the steel works nearby were grimy and the houses equally so as the winds carried dust and smoke everywhere, but the similarities were otherwise remarkable.

For a long while, he sat with his memories until they became too painful. He had shut out the past, including the years of his marriage to Edith, since one fateful summer's day long ago. He was not about to resurrect them now.

Slowly, he raised himself out of the chair, placed the card back onto the darker end of the mantelpiece and shuffled with his empty soup disk into the kitchen.

He tried to shake off his reveries by pottering around. He washed and dried his dish but there was little else to do. He made himself a cup of strong tea but soon he was back in his armchair before his electric fire.

He tried to think of the present. His old friend David was likely to pop in to see him today. He would look forward to that. They had grown up in the same village.

Instantly, he realised his mistake. Thinking of David brought back the image of the village and his past so sharply into his mind, that he became breathless and reached a now trembling hand for his inhaler.

Had not David's son just moved into his and Edith's old house, that very month? Try as he might, he could not stop remembering the past. Sometimes over the years, the horror of what he had done came over him in waves, so much so that at first he had taken to drink to soften his anguish.

Now the card brought everything back with an awful clarity and he sat immobile and stunned, unable to escape from the reality of what had happened.

It had been June 1946 and he had been demobbed from the army after five years active service abroad, during which time he and Edith had seen little of one another. He had been so longing to see her again, however, his homecoming had not been the pleasure he had envisaged.

It was the thought of Edith that had kept up his spirits in the constant clamour of battle. Gunshots and explosions, and the screams of the wounded had stayed with him all the way home. How he had longed for peace and the familiarity of his village.

Although Edith had opened her arms to him at the door, something had changed. He sensed it immediately. At first he reasoned it was because they had not seen each other for so long. It would take time to adjust but it would be alright eventually.

Much had altered though. Edith had begun working in a shop, run by George Evans. She had become the one going out, whilst William had been left at home, unable at first to find a job for himself. Yet even when he managed to get his old job back at the carpenter's yard, the strangeness continued.

He began to watch Edith. Whenever she left for work, she was bubbly and cheerful. He noticed too, that she wore make-up. There was an early morning sparkle about her and although she kissed him as he left for work just before her, it was quick and almost impersonal.

As the weeks went by and became months, they had spent their first Christmas with their parents. With his nephews and nieces around him, he had begun to hope that soon he and Edith would have a family of their own.

★★★

It was the following May that William's world began to collapse. Every Friday evening it had been his practice to go out for a drink with David and some other men friends. On this particular Friday, for some long-forgotten reason, they had decided to go to a small country pub.

William preferred his down-to-earth local, which was always full of familiar faces, but it was David, he recalled now, who had suggested a change.

William now began to breathe more heavily and reached again for his inhaler. David had pushed him in through the door first. The group of friends were jostling and laughing merrily, although as yet had not had so much as a pint.

Then William had stopped short, as the couple nearest the door looked up to see the merrymakers make their entrance. It was then that William and Edith's eyes met, hers with horror and his with shock. For sitting beside her, holding her hand, was her employer George Evans.

The laughter behind him stopped. Then the group caught hold of William's coat and pulled him back outside. William barely remembered what happened next.

With David's, "I'm sorry," ringing in his ears, he had stumbled home.

He had not long to wait. Edith and George had left soon after him, and he tensed as he heard the door latch lift and footsteps coming towards him.

He could not have hit George then if he had tried. He sat on a wooden chair by a dying coal fire and scarcely heard their apologies.

Odd words came back to him but the words that

echoed over and over in his mind were, "We love each other. We are sorry. We love each other."

Without a word, he had gone upstairs to bed. He heard the door slam as George left. Thinking back, he thought Edith had stayed up all night; whilst he lay awake, confused, shocked and unable to think clearly, or absorb what he had seen and heard.

For William, the subsequent days went by in a fog. Towards Edith, he maintained a cold silence. Whenever she tried to talk to him, he would get up, put on his coat and leave the house. All the time, he was thinking and planning.

As June approached it dawned on him that he had been home from the war for a whole year.

"He had," he thought, "gone from one war to another. But the second was only just brewing."

Now he decided he would put his plan into action. First he gave a lad from the village a few pence, together with a message to deliver to George Evans.

"Do not say it is from me," he had cautioned. "It is a surprise."

As he watched the boy scurry off, delighted with the coins in his pocket, William smiled; but not from sharing his young messenger's pleasure, but from his own dark thoughts.

That evening he walked up the hill to the fields that looked down on the village. A farm was perched on its top, from where George Evans bought milk, eggs and butter for his shop.

George too began to ascend the hill, in answer to the message reputedly from the farmer, to discuss prices.

He must have wondered what the farmer was about to propose but he walked unhurriedly, enjoying June's warm evening.

Then George came to an abrupt halt, as he spotted William ahead of him. Promptly changing course, he took a shortcut across the field but still some distance from the farm, he found William blocking his way.

"We need to talk," William said abruptly and pointed to an isolated spot lower down and well out of sight of the farm.

George sauntered downwards, seemingly unperturbed. He was bigger than William and muscular.

"I can handle him," he mused. All the same, it could be an embarrassing encounter. As he walked, he prepared himself for what he would say but no words were to be exchanged. Then, as they passed a large oak tree, William picked up a boulder he had hidden nearby and hit George squarely on the back of his head. He fell to the ground in a heap and with a surprised grunt, and there he lay, still and soundless.

By now, dusk was settling over the hillside. No cows or sheep grazed in this particular field, for it was strewn with boulders and full of deep unexpected crevices.

Now William, in his dark forethought, rolled his unconscious rival down into a deep crevice. He made no attempt to drop anything down to cover the body. No-one ventured near this spot and if George was found, it would look more like an accident that way.

"Number One," he thought grimly and strolled home in the half-light.

The next evening, a Sunday, he suggested to Edith that they go for a walk and have a long talk. Edith seemed willing.

Together, they climbed the same hill in silence.

"Leave the talking until we reach the field," he suggested reasonably. "We'll be able to look down over the whole village on a clear evening like this. I know just the spot."

As he led her across and down the field, he warned her to keep to his right. Unaware of the danger she was in, or of what had transpired the previous day, Edith seemed passive and amenable.

When they neared the spot where he had deposited George, he pretended to hear a cry.

He looked down into the crevice and pointed.

"I think some animal has fallen down there. I can't quite see."

Edith took the bait and squinted down into the crevice but its twisted rocks obscured her view. As she leaned further over, William acted.

"Goodbye. Go to your lover," he snarled, half out of his mind. In an instant, he heard the thud of her body as she tumbled down into the darkness, hitting the uneven sides and bottom of the crevice sickeningly.

William had then gone home. The next day he had told the village that George and Edith had run away. Within days he had moved to a nearby town and his house had been rented out by his landlord almost immediately.

★★★

Now, as William looked back into those dark last days with Edith, tears filled his eyes. Since then he had lived alone. He had worked until he was sixty but rarely went out otherwise.

Then suddenly, his reverie was interrupted by a knock on the door. He looked up, for as usual, David had let himself in.

Together they drank some of the ale David had brought him for Christmas. They chatted quietly until David spotted the Christmas card.

"That reminds me of your old house. My son's house now," he smiled. "He's busy decorating. Oh, by the way. He found this letter, addressed to George Evans, underneath the old dresser you left behind. It must have slipped there when Edith was sweeping the floor. It hasn't been moved in years. Not even by the people who came after you."

William took the still sealed envelope and recognised Edith's elaborate handwriting, with a sinking heart.

"I'll go and make us a sandwich while you read it," suggested David tactfully.

William could hear him whistling in the kitchen. He hesitated and then tore open the envelope with his frail fingers.

He read through the letter in shock. It was to George, saying 'goodbye' as she had just discovered she was having William's baby. Reading on, William realised it had been conceived one night in May, just before he had discovered the couple in the pub.

He had killed his own child!

Quickly, he closed the note and replaced it in the envelope. Then realisation came to him, as he remembered how David had pushed him into the pub that night; a pub David had chosen.

David had known about the affair and he had wanted William to know what was going on. William knew that David had probably meant it to be a kindness. Never-the-less, he had killed his own child because of that night.

A rage boiled up inside him. He beckoned his old friend towards him and caught hold of his tie.

"Hey, you're choking me, Will," spluttered David. "Let go!"

William did not let go. He twisted the tie, and pulled and pulled at it, until David went red in the face.

Then, suddenly, he did let go.

"Read the letter," he said stonily, "but wait until you get home. Goodbye David. We shall not meet again."

Then he closed his eyes, not trusting himself to look at his old friend; the man who had inadvertently cost him his chance of being a father, and forgiving his wife.

"I hope I go soon," he thought, as anger subsided and gave way to self-regret and remorse. Then, with one last glance towards the Christmas card, he fell asleep, he hoped forever.

Rocks That
Sing and Choirs
That Don't

"Well we can't hang about here any longer," said Evan the 'Organ', "or we'll catch our death of cold. This fog has obviously kept the others away. Hywel 'Top-Note' will have to sing treble with young Meurig and Iestyn. That will leave Dai and Mel to sing tenor with Mostyn, and Llew to manage the bass notes on his own. He'll probably drown us all anyway." So saying, Evan peered one last time into the swirling mist, before leading the small group up the rutted pathway to Top Road. Puffing and wheezing slightly in the chill, damp air, he paused beneath a gas lamp, holding out his lantern as the others caught up with him.

It was Christmas Eve, 1921, and although they had no way of knowing it, for some of this small group it was to be their last caroling.

Unsuspectingly, Evan was reflecting that times were hard enough, without the mountain sending down its depressing grey shroud to dampen their spirits even further. Such were his thoughts, as he led the choir through the gate of the first of this row of cottages that huddled together tightly, as if in united defence against the menace of the mountain on whose slopes they rested. Already their clothes were dampened, and their fingertips cold, nevertheless, they sang out lustily, and if 'Good Christian Men Rejoice' fell rather flatly out onto the befogged night air, it was not for any lack of effort on their part.

The time passed pleasantly enough, as the group made its boisterous way along the shadowy row, gazing into ill-lit windows, many of which displayed palm fronds still pressing against the glass, for who, in Pantygraigwen, could afford a Christmas tree. Even so, they saw that some folk had managed to put up the odd trimming or two, and people were happy enough on this Christmas Eve.

The collection box, which Meurig and Iestyn took turns in carrying, was slowly filling with pennies and half-pennies, although Evan knew well they would surely find some buttons and old foreign coins when they came to empty it later.

Evan hurried them on towards the next gate, his fingers fumbling for the latch in their numbness. They were now at number eight, and the mist, far from clearing, clung oppressively low about them, swirling around their ankles like smoke, but alas without the accompaniment of a warm fire's breath.

"Lewis, Llew's son-in-law has just moved in here," Dai informed them. "Not much use singing here, they'll all be down at Llew's having a knees-up, won't they Llew?"

His words fell into the sullen mist as if swallowed up and gained no response.

"That's right, isn't it, boyo?" he asked again, straining his eyes to discern which shadow resembled that of his stocky friend. Now the others were looking round, too.

"Where is Llew?" asked Hywel. "We seem to have left him behind." It was true. Llew was no longer with them.

"He's probably having a crafty sit-down on Teddy Thomas's wall," suggested Dai. "This is no night for a man with a chest like his to be out and about. I'll nip back for him."

"Aye, tell him to go back home," sighed Evan. "Getting money for a new church organ is not worth dying for."

Dai retraced his steps along the way they had come, and seconds later, the subdued thuds of his footfalls had faded away. For a moment, the others waited, straining their ears and eyes for signs of his return, then as if in silent agreement to carry on, they turned into the gate of number nine.

"This fog is going to play havoc with all our chests," spluttered Evan, his throat already feeling effects and showing signs of hoarseness.

"We'll do one or two more and then I think we'll have to call it a day," he added. The thought of soon finishing brought renewed enthusiasm to the group, so that they sang with gusto, accompanying themselves with the stamping of their cold feet in their heavy boots. The result was good.

For the first time that evening, a silver florin dropped into the box, before, with a, "Merry Christmas one and all," Hetty Jenkins quickly shut out, both them and the cold, together.

There was still no sign of Llew or Dai, and their cries of, "Llew, Dai, where are you, boyos?" fell into an unresponsive air. Evan did not know why, but he felt vaguely uneasy and as they stood there, his unease became unfathomable and deep. He felt the stirring of a sinister force around them, giving him the sensation of isolation, as if he and his Sunday choir were being slowly cut off from Pantygraigwen, and indeed from the rest of the world. The entire hamlet was now hidden in the fog, and its smoke muffled their voices even as they spoke one to the other. Whether or not the others were experiencing similar qualms, Evan could not guess. He knew only that the seedling of terror inside him was growing and holding him more and more firmly within its grip. Deliberately he gave a vigorous shake, and made as if to go back.

"I hope that crafty pair aren't having a sneaky cup of cocoa in old Olwen's," Mostyn said gruffly, attempting a laugh at the same time. "If they are sitting there with their feet before her fire, whilst we're out here, chilled to the marrow, there'll be trouble." He grinned to belie his words. "Still, I'd better go and have a look see, just in case Llew's not well. I'll give you a whistle as soon as I find them, and then I'll come straight back here before I do anything else, even if Llew has to be helped home. Alright?"

Mel and the others moved in closer together, as he disappeared in the same direction Dai had taken not long since. Minutes passed, but no shrill whistle cut the silence, and no welcome shuffle of feet came towards them. By now, Evan could see that Mel at least, was strained and apprehensive. The two boys however, just stood there shivering, their thoughts no doubt on the promised festivities of Christmas Day. Hywel remained a passive figure beside him and Evan guessed that the young man's thoughts were probably with young Betty Morgan, the Vicar's daughter.

Then Mel spoke.

"I'll pop you two lads into Hetty's house and ask her to keep an eye on you for a few minutes," he said. "Mind you stay put until we come back for you. Understand?"

Meurig and Iestyn nodded eagerly, still oblivious of the tension amongst their elders, and with a hurriedly whispered sentence to Hetty, Mel saw them safely into the welcoming warmth of her parlour. Then trying to shake off what he regarded as morbid, neurotic fancies, he rejoined his friends.

"Well Mel, well Hywel," Evan said after a pause, his deep voice steady and deliberate. "What do you make of it?"

Hywel's eyes focused suddenly on his companions' strained faces, snapping abruptly out of his pleasant reverie. Now he too felt some inkling of evil lurking in the fog, as the white faces of his friends took on a ghostly appearance.

"I think we should make for home," replied Hywel.

"I'm sure they've gone sneaking off for some sort of joke and they've been longer than they meant – for some reason or other," he added lamely.

"Aye, that's it, boyo," agreed a relieved Mel, "but we'll stick together until we reach Top Road, all the same, and we'll leave the boys where they are. I can come for them later with our Danno when I walk the dog."

So the trio of shadows hurried along the uneven pavements united in their desire to return to the flickering gas lamp at the end of the road. But when they reached its dim pool of light, they suddenly stopped and stood as one, in a communal trance of statues, transfixed, and staring upwards into the snarling mask of the mountain, hovering menacingly above them.

Here the story might have ended, had not Tom Jenkins, of No.1, Top Road, not chosen that moment to look out of his bedroom window. Old man though he is now, he can still be heard to repeat his tale, just as he did in the weeks following that awesome night, to the bewildered villagers and the swarms of reporters who descended upon this hitherto little known hamlet on a South Wales hillside. Surprisingly, Tom's story never wavered, and he kept true to the very first account he gave.

"Just putting young Jim's Christmas stocking on the knob of his bedpost, I was," he said, "when I looked out of the window into the night, and there was Evan the 'Organ,' peering up at the mountain as if he had seen a ghost, and Hywel 'Top-Note' and Mel Jones, just the same." Here he paused dramatically before going on in a hushed voice which brought out all the mystery of his strange story. "They crossed the road towards my house, and then disappeared along the track. I ran into the back bedroom, and there they were, going up the mountain, one behind the other, just as if they were sleep walking. I opened the window despite the night being so cold. 'Where are you off to, boys?' I shouted. 'Funny time for a picnic, isn't it?' But they didn't even turn their heads. They just kept on going." He paused again for breath. "Then it was I saw," he said, sounding like an actor from some old melodrama at Ponty Town Hall, "a great spluttering ball of green fire, pulsing away at the very top of the mountain, and before I knew what was happening, it was glowing right inside my bedroom. I closed my eyes, don't ask me why, and I slammed the window shut, and drew the curtains as fast as I could, I can tell you."

This then is Tom's story, and his listeners still shudder as he describes that beckoning light. As to Evans and his "boys," well to most people, they are lost, gone without trace. But young Meurig and Iestyn, both grown men now, have strong ideas of their own. Didn't they find a new outcrop of rocks huddling on the mountain side, and didn't they sit on them only to be pinched and grazed as if being urged away? Was it really only the wind that moaned through the crevices, a moan that sounded so much like the deep bass of Llew at his rumbling best? Somehow, neither believed it was, but they kept these secret thoughts to themselves, a last secret to share with Evan, Mel, Hywel, Mostyn, Dai and Llew. One thing was sure. Neither ever ventured out singing carols on the mountain of Pantygraigwen again. Nor would they even venture out on Christmas Eve. Each was convinced that the light had meant to beckon them too on that fateful night. Each felt that one day, that small huddle of stones would be complete. They were fighting the inevitable maybe, but fight they would.

POSTSCRIPT:

EXCERPT FROM THE PONTYPRIDD OBSERVER.
CHRISTMAS EVE, 1942.

Mr. Tom Jenkins, of No.1, Top Road, Pantygraigwen, was arrested for being drunk and disorderly outside the Tymawr Hotel, last evening. Police said he was incoherent and unsteady on his feet, but spent the night at the police station at his own request.

"He seemed in the grip of fear," reported Inspector Gwyn Jones, "and insisted that he must not be taken home until Christmas Day. However, none of my men wanted to earn a poor reputation for jailing a hitherto respectable citizen over the Christmas holiday, so we insisted he be released this morning."

Excerpt from the Pontypridd Observer. 3ʀᴅ January 1942.

The body of Mr. Tom Jenkins of No.1, Top Road, Pantygraigwen, was discovered by a neighbour, on Christmas morning. It appears that Mr. Jenkins went for a walk up the local mountainside, when a group of boulders became dislodged and rolled down on to him. He was killed instantly. Local villagers report hearing a strange sound at the time, almost like that of carol singers.

Excerpt from Pontypridd Observer. 21ˢᴛ June 1942.

Yesterday afternoon, two men from Pantygraigwen lost their lives when a car in which they were travelling left the mountain road and plunged some forty feet into the valley below. The two men, Meurig Lewis and Iestyn Morgan, had been returning from a choir practice at a church in the adjoining valley. Initial investigations suggest the road conditions were good at the time. The precise reason for the accident is not yet known.

ONE BLIND MOUSE

"She's such a frump!" Muffled by the thickness of her bedroom door, the hotel chambermaid's words dimly penetrated Lisa's dulled senses. For some reason, the words began to echo and re-echo in hypnotic sing-song rhythm. They hammered into her tired brain like that old nursery rhyme she had sung so often as a child, when life had been light and full of hope.

"Three blind mice. Three blind mice.
She's such a frump. She's such a frump.
We'll cut off her tail with a carving knife,
Yes, cut off her tail with a carving knife.
Such a frump. Such a frump."

Lisa crossed the room and sat before the elegant Queen Anne style dressing table. Purposefully, she stared into the gleaming mirror, and gazed at her reflection, long and hard. Far from lulling her into her familiar daily stupor, the rhythm of the words jarred in their repeated cruelty. Truth pierced the seemingly impregnable armour of shock that had cocooned her for so long. Now, for the first time in five years, she was becoming aware – aware of herself. Her name came to her in a sudden rush of blood to her head. She was Lisa Davidson, wife of the dark, strikingly handsome accountant, Peter James Davidson. Peter, who had become more and more successful as the years rolled by for him. Rolled for him, but yawned for her, she mused, else why was she feeling so desperately tired?

She gave a start as her attention turned back to the face in the mirror. Out of that mocking glass peered a dull, drab stranger. Small shock waves shivered through her thin frame as her dark eyes registered themselves, shadowed and haunted and set in yellowed sockets. At the sight of her crepe-like colourless skin, she closed her eyes in horror, so that she missed the deep red flush that spread across her hollow cheeks.

For a long while she sat immobile with her eyes staying firmly closed. She pictured herself with the beautiful oval face that Peter had loved to caress with his long, slender fingers. Her skin had been aglow then, creamy soft and smooth. Her eyes, more often than not had been full of laughter and so alive, whilst her hair – how Peter had loved to stroke its thick chestnut tresses. Her hair had been her greatest asset, its coppery tints catching the sun and shining so that passers-by in the streets, would turn their heads and smile. Now the silken strands had become limp straggles of grease, a fitting frame for this lifeless ghost. With a deep sigh, she acknowledged that no blink of eye or toss of head, would shake away the mirror's unrelenting image.

Slowly, she opened her eyes and at the same time, the rhyme came back, incessant and forceful.

"Such a frump! Such a frump." It was true. It was more than true she acknowledged wryly. It was the understatement of all time. How could she have let herself become this pathetic creature? No wonder that Peter was easing away from her, slipping further and further into becoming a dream figure. How could she expect him to go on loving her, when she was looking like this? She struggled to remember when the two of them had last spent an evening together. If she were not careful, she would lose him!

Stronger shock waves swelled through her, jolting her at last into full consciousness. Wildly she gripped the edge of the dressing table as fear swept through her.

"Please God," she begged, "let there be something left to salvage."

Lisa had no way of knowing how long she sat there, gaining strength and equanimity, but gradually her heartbeat steadied, determination replaced the fear and she began to try to think positively. It was up to her. No one else could work a miracle for her. She was not really aware that for the first time in years, the morning would not stretch unnoticed into afternoon, and further unmarked into the fog of evening. Suddenly there was much to do. Time was short and she must act quickly. She must put things right whilst there was still a chance. She must put herself in order.

In the background of her thoughts the nursery rhyme still rocked on, but she urged herself to ignore it.

"Don't look back, Lisa," she admonished herself. "It's your future and it's beckoning you now." Reaching into her handbag, she withdrew a slim ivory notecase with a gold pencil attached. Ignoring the mirror still before her, she began to write. She was surprised to find her fingers were stiff as if writing had become an unfamiliar task. Strange tingling and weakness joined the stiffness, as if the fingers were facing unaccustomed effort. Already too, her brain was beginning to tire again, as if it were quite unused to the effort of making coherent thought. For a few minutes she persevered, gaining a little strength as she went along. Then when her list seemed complete, she read it through with tired satisfaction.

Choosing the first priority was easy, a visit to the hairdresser's was paramount. She would try Jean-Pierre first. For a while, daydreams took over, as she remembered the first time she and Peter had come to this sleepy Cotswold town, set high in the hills and deep in the peace of its countryside. Jean-Pierre had arranged her hair, piling it high up on the crown of her head, and immediately afterwards, Peter had entered a quaint antique shop a few yards away, emerging with the turquoise pendant.

"It will show off your beautiful, slender neck," he had said proudly. Where was it now? She could not remember wearing it since – her mind fogged. Deep within her, a disturbing memory of terror, followed by sharp, final grief tormentingly fleeted into her wanderings, but it had shrugged away, before she could grasp it. Her thoughts strayed back to Jean-Pierre. She struggled unsuccessfully to picture his face, but she could recall his voice with its caressing accent.

"Your hair has such movement, Madame. You must promise me that you will never have it permed. You are so fortunate. Many women would pay many pounds for hair such as this." Lisa smiled, secure in the knowledge of his obvious admiration and sincerity. A visit to Jean-Pierre would definitely come first. She glanced back down at her list and read on.

In her wavy handwriting, she had scribbled, "Book in at Great Chester Health Farm." She shuddered at the enormity of the task she was about to place before the staff there. She shuddered again, as she realised what an effort it would be for to tackle any of these ventures. She would, of course have to explain away her strange looks, an illness perhaps. She frowned. Had she indeed been ill? She tried to concentrate on the past, on yesterday, on the last weekend, but her bewilderment only increased. Dimly, she envisaged long hours spent in a hospital bed, pale nurses in ghostly white bending over her, sometimes kindly and smiling, occasionally exasperated and impatient. It was all so indistinct.

Wisely, she came back to the present. Yes, she must definitely have been ill. Once she had had her hair fixed, she would look much better. She walked unsteadily the few steps to a side table by her bed. She must have been very ill indeed. Her legs would hardly support her and her head began to swim with the effort. She opened a magazine. Perhaps she would find a style she would like, one that Peter would admire, but before she opened the pages, the date across the top hit her with new force of shockwaves.

"October 29th. 1979?" Surely it was only 1974? Her head began to throb and her nerve ends tingled with tiny stabs of pain, but nothing seemed to stay for long and these new disturbances were dismissed as she thumbed urgently though the pages. She had forgotten to look for styles. Instead, she turned fumbling, to the adverts and soon found the number she required.

"Great Chester Health Farm. Good morning. How may I help you?" The voice purred quietly into her ear, giving Lisa a peculiar sensation, as if she were unused to conversation. She struggled to speak, but found the words strangling themselves within her throat, and panic took over.

"Good morning," the voice repeated, loosing a little of its smoothness in the repetition. "How may I help you?" Lisa cleared her throat awkwardly and found her voice.

"Have you any immediate vacancies?" she asked, her own voice unpleasantly loud and rasping to her ears. "I would like to stay for a whole week, if possible," she added, her voice tailing off faintly.

"Have you availed yourself of our services before, Madame?" asked the voice a little pompously.

"Yes. This is Lisa Davidson. I visited your farm only –" she was about to say 'last year,' but the date on the magazine floated before her eyes again. Cautiously, she amended her words, "some little while ago. Sophie will remember me I'm sure."

"Sophie is away on vacation, Mrs. Davidson." The voice had begun to purr again now. "I am sure she will be delighted to see you on her return. I'm afraid the earliest appointment I can give you will be in two weeks' time."

Lisa settled the arrangements quickly and abruptly, her nerve failing her and making her bring the conversation to a speedy close.

Should she ring Jean-Paul or surprise him? She decided on the latter, confident that he would give her his immediate attention. Her thoughts turned towards clothes.

She needed a good, but elegant suit and a long romantic evening dress. Excitement welled up inside her, taking away the feeling of lethargy. Energy flowed back into her limbs.

What colours should she choose? Peter liked her in soft green.

"It matches your eyes, darling," he would say. Yes, perhaps green would be a good choice for the suit and maybe muted colours for the dress. They would give tone to her colourless cheeks and avoid a clash with her hair.

Her hair. She grimaced as the truth hit her again. Those lovely red tones no longer burnished her hair. Indeed, it not only lacked the fire of its former colour, but of life as well. Perhaps, for once, she should choose something vivid, exotic even, to compensate until her hair became restored to something like its former colour.

She wondered what clothes she had brought with her to this town. Was she on holiday? Vaguely she wondered why Peter was not with her, but the puzzlement did not stay with her, but flitted in and out of her thoughts like quicksilver. Confused, she was unable to concentrate long enough to contain more than the occasional shaft of anxiety of her memory loss.

She turned to the wardrobe and opened it tentatively. There, hanging lopsidedly on a flimsy hanger, was one smart, silk dress peeping beneath a matching coat. It was too thin for this season, if indeed it really was October. She stared at it incredulously. Where were the rest of her clothes? Still a little unbalanced, she took the coat and dress out of the wardrobe. Both were of pale mustard, a colour which had always suited her well. Her glance went back to the window. Outside, the sun was giving the avenue of trees a bright, welcoming hue, but even so she sensed the cold crispness of the Autumn. She decided that the clothes shops must come first after all.

At the back of the wardrobe she found a pair of shoes, more suitable she thought for an afternoon trip to see her best friend Hetty, than for a holiday away from it all. For a split second or so, she wondered if perhaps she had been so ill that she was still in hospital, but again her mind rejected the possibility and she found herself wondering about Hetty. When had she last seen her? Just as she felt she was about to remember, the picture became hazy, and not wanting to prolong the nightmare of wondering, Lisa shook the image off. The memory of her best friend faded and she began feverishly to dress.

A little later, she found herself behaving quite oddly, opening the door tentatively and peering round. It was as if her life depended upon her remaining unobserved. Although she recognised the strangeness of her movements, some inner sense of preservation warned her that this was how she should behave.

From somewhere quite near, she could hear sounds of trolleys squeaking. She deduced that some guests were still being served lunch in their rooms. She herself always insisted on her meals being served in private, although she could not recall why. The question fleeted by without an answer as she hesitantly tip-toed down the corridor.

She found herself looking down a stone stairway. She was glad of the flimsy shoes for they made little sound, but was surprised to see how weak and wobbly she felt, even though the heels were not too high. Slowly she went down the stairs, holding on to the wooden rail with trembling hands.

Half way down, as the stairs curled round hiding her from anyone who might be passing by above, she sank to the cold stone and rested. She had no idea how long she stayed there, but no one came along. She could hear the distant whine of the lifts going up and down relentlessly. She thanked God for them. Only fools would use the staircase when the lifts were in such good working order. She allowed herself a wry smile.

It was some time later when she found herself leaning against a store window in the High Street. She felt exhausted and quite unreal. She had no recollection of walking there and felt as if she were floating in a world of muffled sounds and misted faces.

After a while, her vision began to clear and some strength came back into her legs. Even so, she felt unable to push open the heavy swing doors of the dress salon, but waited until another shopper opened them. Then she followed her inside. Immediately, she felt the comforting warmth of central heating and moving slowly, she found herself in the Model Gowns Department. She did not recognise the door, but it was obviously a store of some class and one of which Peter was bound to approve.

The salon's deep carpeting added to her sense of unreality and she dismissed Peter from her thoughts as she moved soundlessly through to the central displays. Her sense of dissociation was broken suddenly as the strident voice of a dissatisfied customer querulously cut across the subdued atmosphere. The customer emerged from a curtained cubicle and sailed forth on the tide of her indignation, brushing aside a harassed assistant and rudely passing too close to Lisa. Lisa's plans were re-awakened. She drifted towards the displayed gowns and let the tirade fade into the background. As her thin fingers stroked the lovely garments, she felt a thrill of pleasure suffuse her.

Taking a beautiful saffron dress in softest chiffon down from its rail, she marvelled at its lightness and beauty. It had an ethereal quality and she knew she would look no further. This was a dress to make all heads turn. Surely Peter would love her again when he saw her floating towards him in this.

Why had she thought 'again?' Peter had always loved her, hadn't he? Had they had a quarrel? She struggled to remember, but already her thoughts had drifted back towards the dress. She draped it over her arm, and paying no attention to the gowns draping the plaster models, she moved a little swifter towards the daywear room.

When she reached the rails, she was taken aback. There was a good assortment of suits, but they were all terribly long. Glancing around her, she became suddenly aware that the few shoppers near her were wearing skirts well below their knees. Instantly, she felt gawkish, as she saw how her bony knees protruded beneath the coat. She felt or imagined eyes staring at her, but at that moment, the disgruntled customer chose to come storming back through the salon, garrulously informing everyone of her opinion of the service, or rather lack of it, that she had received. Thankful that attention had switched to this large, rather florid lady, Lisa moved along the rail.

Tiredness swept over her as she tried to choose between a mulberry in softest courtelle, or a knitted chocolate brown. She was disappointed to find that all the greens were too dark and some too heavy in weight too. Weakness overcame her again. She knew she would be too weary to try anything on today.

She was unaware of how long she had stood there, before she noticed she was attracting the attention of a tall, blond-haired gentleman across the room. Nicely suited, his hooded blue eyes seemed to be staring at her with undisguised interest. Lisa forgot the revelations of the mirror in her bedroom. She forgot the ugly secrets it had revealed. She felt only his admiration, just as she had felt Peter's, so many, many times in the past. She was thinking of Peter as she finally drifted out of the store, her new purchases flung carelessly over her arm, lightening her step and warming her day.

★★★

The Police Station was hot and stuffy and appeared to be surrounded by people with colds. Lisa registered the constant blowing of noses and sniffing. Somewhere, in a room elsewhere, someone had a persistent hacking cough. Suddenly, the coughing seemed to merge into the nursery rhyme again. She found herself singing, in a weak high voice that she didn't recognise as her own, at all.

"Was I a blind mouse?
Was I a blind mouse?
But I cut off their tails with a carving knife,
Yes, I cut off their tails with a carving knife,
Did you ever see such a thing in your life as
One blind mouse. One blind mouse."

The words churned over and over in her mind in step with the distant coughing. She found the words oddly comforting and began to rock herself gently and quite unconsciously to their rhythm.

A vague figure thrust a hot mug of tea into her stiff fingers and she warmed her hands around it, but her jerky movements caused the hot liquid to spill over onto the blanket someone had kindly placed over her knees. A young man took it gently from her. Lisa thought he seemed very interested in her.

"It's no good," she wanted to say. "I am already spoken for. I have eyes only for Peter," but she had no wish to be cruel, so she settled for a pitying smile.

Vaguely she wondered why he did not smile back. She wished he would go away. He was spoiling her singing. Other people appeared to be surrounding her too. She sensed that they wanted her to say something, but she was too tired for conversation. She wanted them all to go away and leave her in peace. Finally, their voices dimmed as she began to doze.

Roderick Allen, the Store Manager, settled into a chair across the table from her. Reluctantly he took his eyes off her and addressed the sergeant standing by the door.

"It would appear that this lady has been unwell for some considerable time, Sergeant," he said decisively. "Please understand that I have not brought her into the station to be charged. I thought you would be able to find out who she is. I hope that you will agree that in the circumstances a charge would be most inappropriate and indeed inhuman. This poor lady, was without doubt, completely unaware of her actions. My assistants felt badly about bringing her to my attention. Indeed, if it had not been for a time-demanding recalcitrant customer, they would have sought to help her. It was obvious from the outset, that no money would be offered for the garments she was choosing. They contacted me and we then waited for her to walk off the premises, so that we could have the authority to detain her. We brought her here purely to seek help for her."

Throughout his long, rather pompous speech, Mr. Allen seemed anxious to justify his actions, but his concern seemed genuine and his blue eyes drew an answering sympathy in those of the sergeant. He now noticed that they had been joined by Inspector Davies, who hastened to assure the young man of their support. In truth, he had been shocked by the haggard unreality of the young woman's face.

"We are trying to trace her now, Mr. Allen," he started. "But we have very little to go by. Apart from this list and one or two cosmetics which appear to have been unused for some time, her handbag was empty. However, we have managed to contact this fellow here," he pointed to the list, "one Jean Pierre, alias Albert Johnson," he added with a grin. "He is on his way here. We have also contacted this Health Farm. The Receptionist confirms that she had a strange call regarding a booking, earlier today. This could have come from our friend here. The girl says the voice was weak and the lady spoke in disjointed sentences. More importantly though, she had given a name which was that of an old customer and had claimed to know the proprietress by her Christian name. The latter is on holiday but can be quickly traced, should our Jean Pierre fail to recognise our mystery woman."

At that moment, he was interrupted by the entrance of a fresh-complexioned young man with dark silky hair effeminately cut. He sported a silk shirt and tight jeans, and at his bony wrists gold bracelets clanked irritatingly. Formalities over, Jean Pierre looked hard at the lady resting her head against a tea stained wall, and shook his head.

"Sorry, I'm afraid I can't help. I have never seen this lady before."

"Look again," urged the inspector. "Does the name Mrs. Davidson help?" he added, giving the name provided by the receptionist. The young man turned his head with an affected flick of his curls. Then he gave the vacant eyed lady before him a closer scrutiny and the name brought incredulous recognition. His distress was genuine.

"My God," he whispered, "she was so lovely. Her hair was gorgeous, absolutely gorgeous, a mass of copper that danced in the light." He leant forward as if to touch the dank dull hair before him but could not bring himself to do so. Instead, he sank down on the bench and began to speak, still in that awed semi-hush of a man in shock.

"You know the story don't you?" he asked, and as each man shook his head, he began to speak whilst they listened with growing incredulity and shock.

Back in her room in the psychiatric ward of the private nursing home where she had lain inert and unresponsive for almost five years, the nurses were receiving new orders. Absolute security now became of utmost importance for the patient was no longer in a catatonic state. From now on, all bolts must be secured without fail and at every entry and exit to and from her room.

A grim looking nurse emerged from her room, and was about to fasten two heavy bolts, when Roderick Allen, the Store Manager, appeared and stopped her with a shake of his head. The face of his shoplifter haunted him and he had, on impulse, accompanied the police to the institution without protest from them.

"May we go in for a moment?" he asked.

"The three of you?" she queried in a surprisingly soft voice, looking from him to the sergeant and the uniformed officer. When the sergeant nodded, she left them with a last warning. "Be on your guard." The policemen noticed she did not go far away and they let themselves in with some apprehension.

Sensing that this was a special moment for the young shop manager, the sergeant indicated to the constable that perhaps they should stay near the door, tactfully keeping as far out of earshot, as possible in the limited space. Despite its bars, the room was pleasant, its window looking out onto a garden, fringed with the beautiful russets of trees in Autumn.

Lisa watched Roderick walk in.

"So handsome," she smiled. Then her mouth twisted. Peter had been handsome. Peter had been handsome but unfaithful too. Men were all the same. This was the man who had smiled at her in the shop. Well she would teach this one a lesson too, just as she had taught Peter. Her face creased for an instant into such a snarl of a smile that Roderick felt distressed, but her thoughts had slid away from him now, back to Peter.

She had planned the accident so well, from that first moment when she had unexpectedly walked into Peter's office just as he was fitting a turquoise pendant around his pretty secretary's neck. She remembered the ugly flush which had spread across that pretty face and Peter's too as they became aware of her standing there, watching them. Peter's face had reddened too, but even then she had been cunning. Even in her shock, she had known she would one day make him pay.

Lisa had let the months go by, with Peter relaxed and sure of her forgiveness. Then Lisa had called upon her memory and her scientific training. She had brought Peter a gift. She had sprinkled it in his coffee before cheerfully kissing him farewell. Then she had watched him drive away, her gift seeping through his bloodstream. She had felt neither remorse or distress, nothing but triumph that her's was the gift of death.

Her reverie paused as she acknowledged the interest in the eyes of the young man standing by her chair. She gave him her prettiest smile. One day, she would give this man a gift too.

Later, as Roderick crossed the car park with the two policemen, his step seemed lighter and more confident that when they had arrived.

"I've a feeling she will get better," he asserted. "She gave me quite a bright –" he paused, for you could hardly call that grimace a smile. Yet he was convinced that that's what she had meant it to be. "she gave me quite a bright look," he amended. "The shock of coming out of her catatonic state must have done her good. You know, she has rather lovely eyes still. As she gets well, who knows, she might become beautiful again."

The sergeant glanced at him uneasily, but Roderick went on.

"You can see she had something once," he enthused. "I might pop over to see her once in a while. It might help and I do feel rather responsible for bringing her to you and all that."

As the car drove off, the constable shook his head. "Has he forgotten that she poisoned her husband? Has he forgotten that she planned it cold bloodedly for months, kissing him goodbye each morning as if all was forgiven? Can he be that naive?"

The sergeant joined him in the car. He too was concerned. The young man appeared to be over sensitive and easily influenced. Perhaps later, when her memory had faded a little, he would meet up with Roderick and give him a friendly word of advice. However, as the car sped back to the station, both, men's thoughts turned to other pressing matters, and Lisa and Roderick were forgotten.

After their departure, a long, black shadow crept over the car park, spreading wide prongs towards the old oak. The tree's branches shivered as if to shake the shadows away, but they hung there except for one finger of shade which had followed the headlights of one departing car far into the evening. Back in her 'hotel room', Lisa's brain whirled with plans. The dark finger of shade and her dark thoughts merged, reaching out towards the young man at the wheel, into his future – unless a miracle were to happen, and of course, sometimes miracles do.

MISSING FROM HOME

CHAPTER ONE

Fear pervaded the town of Winnowsty, like smoke slowly seeping from an underground fire. For months discontented youths and a handful of tough, bizarre looking girls with weird hairstyles and army reject clothes, had been drifting through the town in twos and threes, joining up with others as unemployment reached a new high in the Midlands.

Now the twosomes were rare. In their place had come the gangs. Aimlessly, rowdily and destructively they roamed through the shopping centres, car parks and suburbs. Always, in their wake, lay the smashed and the shattered, the broken and the bruised, the defiled and the defaced.

The debris they left behind them was more than just evidence of frustrated boredom. In its remains, it spelled out a creeping, callous indifference to the feelings of man, woman or child.

Over the past year, the disturbances had grown both in violence and in number. The elderly, the fragile and the lonely had become targets for young thugs, looking for kicks against a society which held no meaningful place for them. Many people no longer walked the streets with the ease of familiarity. Instead they ventured into them with timidity and a wariness that hastened their erstwhile leisurely shopping outings.

Something needed to be done. Each Sunday, church bells would ring out their melodious welcome to the services. However, few but the handful of regulars attended, sitting amongst many empty seats which made spoken and sung words echo around the emptiness.

In one such church, the church of St. John's, the vicar frequently spoke of goodwill and peace, of love and fellowship, offering temporary comfort to those inside. Unbeknown to him, a tape recorder was whirring, quietly marking his words for a future time and a different audience. It was the beginning of a secret fight-back against a lack of respect and concern for people in general.

Each Saturday, a tall man would saunter through the local park, his Alsatian dog Max trotting obediently at his heels. He did not carry a tape recorder. It was safely stowed elsewhere but it would not be silent for long. Casually, he traversed the long pathways, bordered by heavily scented bushes and then more purposefully, he and Max made their way across the park, past the children's playground, his cool grey eyes hidden beneath his sunglasses, flickering here and there, missing nothing. Walking on, he had taken in every detail, the obvious and the obscure, whilst his faithful dog walked steadily on, as if following an unseen line. Occasionally, he would lift soft brown eyes and gaze up at his master with devotion.

At around the same time, a slightly stockier man was crossing the playing fields at the opposite end of the park. He was alone. As he too strolled along, he dodged a football fast coming his way and smiled at the lads enjoying their innocent game. He made his way towards the nature reserve, and then around its fence, walking as unerringly as the first man, towards his own destination.

Finally, he stopped beside the Victorian bandstand. Then, picking up a metal chair, he mounted the steps with it and set it down inside the stand. Once seated, he took a paperback novel out of his jacket pocket and soon, he appeared to be deeply engrossed in his reading, but for some reason, he too was wearing sunglasses.

By now, the first man and his dog, had reached the brow of a hill at the park's western edge. From here the park fell gently away, levelling off occasionally to provide a wide picnic area, and then rolling down to where the tennis courts and swimming pool lay sprawled. Finding a broad tree trunk on which to lean, he and Max settled onto the grass, Max squatting beside him.

From this vantage point, they had an overall view of this side of the park. At first, the afternoon passed uneventfully, although the emptiness of the more popular areas emphasised the nervousness of the townspeople. True, there were about a hundred or more in the park's total area, but normally, on a warm summer's day like this, there would have been more like five hundred. As it was, a local cricket match accounted for most of those present, along with a few dads kicking soccer balls across the playing fields with their youngsters chasing to return them. There were some brave souls with pushchairs risking taking the short cut home through the park, but otherwise, it was very quiet for a Saturday afternoon.

No one paid any attention to either of the men, except for one curious, small lad who noticed that the man in the bandstand was slow at turning over his pages. Idly wondering why, he surmised that the man was a slow reader.

"Just like wot I am in school," he giggled. "He should be in the remedial class wiv me." Then he forgot all about the man and went on chucking up handfuls of grass in the air with his chubby hands. Suddenly, he spotted his friends and was racing away across to them. The strange man was forgotten.

CHAPTER TWO

It was five o'clock now and the light was beginning to fade. Faint shadows spread over parts of the green fields and the footballs bounced for the last time that afternoon. Thoughts of tea time overtook the lure of the game and soon the playing fields were empty. People from all over the park were heading towards the gates, fanning out towards the western and southern exits.

Up on the hill the first man remained statue-like, although anyone close by would have been able to detect him easing his foot positions with military like precision. The sunglasses remained in place, despite the hill now being bathed in one wide triangular shadow.

Similarly, the second man appeared to be deceptively still. Occasionally, he would glance up and look around, but in a casually indifferent way.

It was about this time that a third man emerged. He appeared to be late for an appointment, as he hastened along the paths towards the play area. Approaching the swings, he swerved and after a furtive glance around, he hid in the rhododendron bushes, just yards from the swings for toddlers.

There he stopped, haste no longer being a requirement. Briskness was replaced by immobility. Only a handful of children remained and most of them were having their last swings of the day.

From his high vantage point, the man on the hill took out some field glasses with which he scanned the park in a slow arc, turning from left to right. He could see both the man in the bandstand and a hint of the other in the bushes, but he did not keep the glasses trained on them. Instead, he moved them steadily back towards the main park entrance.

Just then, two young girls with bright canvas bags on their shoulders, came swinging through the gates. The muscles in his arms tensed beneath his light jacket, as he judged them to be about fourteen years old, or maybe a little older.

The watcher kept his glasses trained on them as they made their leisurely way past the bowling greens and putting kiosk. They were heading towards the bandstand and the open parkland beyond.

As they passed the man still sitting on the by now uncomfortable chair, they gave him a quick glance but dismissed him as too old when he glanced up from his book. As they ambled along, they giggled and chattered in shrill voices, whilst keeping their eyes open for any good looking boys that might come their way.

Now the dozing Max pricked up his long ears, as he sensed his master was tensing and more alert. He stretched himself and began to pace backwards and forwards, rubbing against the watcher's knees.

"Steady, Max," the man admonished. "It's early yet. Settle down, there's a good lad." The dog obediently did as he was told, seeking out the same spot as before, which he had warmed all afternoon.

A few minutes after the girls had passed by, the second watcher took out of his pocket, a small mirror, as if to check his dark, shining hair was in place. Then, picking up the chair, he replaced it in the rows outside the stand and began to walk briskly in the same direction as the girls. When they came into sight however, he slowed to a stroll.

Up on the hill, Max and his master had seen the glint of light on glass. The dog remained where he was, but now that the signal had come sooner than expected, he was taut and ready to spring.

His master was busy, focussing his glasses on to the side park entrance. Here, the land was bordered by a shabby run-down suburb, which could easily degenerate into slums in a few more years of unemployment.

It was through this entrance that a group of youths came swaggering in. Pushing and jostling each other playfully, they did not appear to be a threat to anyone. In any case, no one crossed their path.

Still, the watcher kept his glasses trained on them as they made their noisy way towards the recreation ground. Turning the field glasses slightly, he saw that the girls, still shadowed by the second man, would be sure to cross the path of the lads unless they changed direction shortly. His hidden eyes followed them as far as the playground.

By now, only one child remained on the swings. Small and about eight years old, he changed now to the roundabout and was happily whizzing round, using one shabby shoe to propel him faster. When the girls approached, they ignored him and sat themselves on the larger swings, still giggling and teasing each other about boys from their school.

From the distance, the watcher in the bushes could hear the sounds of raucous laughter as the youths came nearer. He heaved a sigh of relief a moment later, as the man from the putting kiosk came and the small boy ran eagerly towards him, his face earnest with pleasure.

"Hi, Dad," he cried in delight. "What has Mum got for our tea?"

"Wait and see," laughed his dad, picking him up and swinging him round. Then they hurried off together, hand in hand.

The man in the bushes was glad, one less to worry about. He did not move until the girls had left the swings and moved on towards the fields. The girls were disappointed to find the fields empty. They had hoped to make watching football an excuse to get to know a likely lad or two.

Turning hopefully around, they spotted the man from the bandstand.

"Hey, there's the reading man from the bandstand," laughed one. "Do you think he fancies us?" and they squealed with high pitched laughter. They both thought he looked old enough to be their granddads.

The watcher would not have been flattered for he was only in his late twenties! He did not return the girls' interest, not that they were bothered. Any thoughts of him had been fleeting and shallow, born out of boredom.

The man disappeared from their view. Unbeknown to the girls, he was not far away, leaning lazily against a convenient tree. His eyes were not on the girls and he was straining to scan the distance from where he could hear the rough bantering of the gang. He was trying to pinpoint their position.

Three watchers, disguised in dark glasses; two young girls, innocently looking for an adventure; and the occasional dog walker, spelt an almost deserted park apart from the converging youths. Their presence brought a pervading sense of malice.

The girls were aware now of the voices of boys or young men. They sounded friendly, as if they were having fun. As of one thought, the girls drifted towards the promise of young male company. They were neither promiscuous nor sophisticated, just two young girls, their heads full of romantic dreams, eager to find one of their paper heroes in the weeklies, come to life.

Behind them, on two sides they were being stalked by two of the watchers, whilst the man on the rise began to descend the hill with long strides. He had used his mirror to warn his friends and all three faces were now grim and determined, although each one hoped their fears were misguided and that all would be well.

Max bounded alongside his master, zig-zagging from left to right in his delight at having some exercise at last. They had been on the hill for almost two hours.

Ahead of them, the youths had become aware of the sounds of girlish squeals. One greasy haired youth broke away from the others and ran up onto a bank. From there he soon came whooping down and the gang turned directly towards the unsuspecting girls, who were now in sight as they rounded a curving path.

The girls, Patti and Jude, caught sight of the boys at the same time. As only the first two boys came around the path, the girls shyly smiled. But the smiles grew strained and tense, as more and more youths appeared – skinheads, punks and others, all in long thin drainpipes or dirty beer-stained jeans. Some wore black leather jackets with sinister brass studs embossed on them. Somehow the studs looked like the ugly spots of adolescence. At their wrists too, they wore wide, leather straps with matching studs.

Jude's face had gone white with fear, but she whispered earnestly to her friend that they should not run.

"Just keep on walking and ignore them," she muttered. "They may not bother us."

"Jude, I'm scared," whispered Patti back. "Let's go."

But it was too late to turn around. As they came face to face with the lads, they feared trouble was about to engulf them. Warnings from their mums came to mind, and thinking of their mums and dads suddenly made them want to cry. Then to their disbelief, the youths parted and let them pass with no more than a jibe and a jostle or two.

Slowly, the colour came back into the girls' cheeks. For a while they hurried, but gradually relaxed. Allowing themselves a quick glance back, they saw that the youths had settled into a huddle on the grass, and all thoughts of romance now gone, they were eager to get home.

The early evening was still warm and scented from the many plants. As the light began to dim further, sudden frantic flashes of light danced across the borders, coming from three directions in quickly succeeding sequences. The light startled the birds, causing them to fly out from the bushes in a fluster.

In turn, their rustling startled the girls, but the warning was insufficient. Before they had time to register alarm, they were grabbed from behind and thrust into the dark, scented cluster of branches and twisting roots. Strong arms grasped them cruelly and sharp knees dug into them as they were yanked further into the darkness of the bushes' undermass.

Both girls screamed before finding themselves gagged by dirty, roughened hands. Struggling to free themselves, they kicked out and bit the thumbs of their assailants, but more hands came about to tear at their clothing.

Patti mercifully passed out. Jude, terrified out of her wits almost, fought wildly, kicking at the squirming bodies trying to reach her properly in the undergrowth. A great weariness descended over her as she found her legs held and the hopelessness of struggling penetrated her hysteria. She too was on the point of collapse.

It was then that the weight was lifted off her, as if by some supernatural force. There was startled swearing and shouts of indignation turning to fear as there came snarling sounds of a dog biting flesh and into bone.

Jude realised that the shrieks were no longer hers. The cries of pain came from the hoarse throats of youths. Although arms and legs still seemed to kick out at her, she knew that she was only on the fringe and the kicks were without depth. Soon the sounds of violence had moved away from her and the bushes. She found herself alone with Patti in the darkness of the undergrowth.

She looked down at her mussed but unbroken clothing and was shuddering uncontrollably, when two strong arms lifted her gently out into the light, and a deep soothing voice sought to comfort her.

"It's alright, lass. You and your friend have had a frightening few moments, but no real harm has been done." Not physically, he thought, but who knows what the lasting effects will be on their minds.

Sitting her down onto the grass, he went back into the bushes to rescue Patti, who was just coming out of her faint. He began to ease her out, but she struggled in protest. Those thugs were outside and she could not bear to have them looking at her. She felt degraded and ashamed beyond belief, but the voice spoke reassuringly.

"Those hoodlums have gone. My friends, not to mention my dog, are seeing to them. The others have cowardly run away. You need see no one but the Park Keeper. He has already phoned for the police and an ambulance.

"I don't want to go to hospital. I just want to go home," interrupted Jude, who was now crying weakly and still shaking from shock. Beside her, Patti was incoherent but nodding her head in agreement.

The tall man helped both girls onto a wooden bench, where they huddled together for comfort. As he went to move away, they panicked.

"Please don't leave us", cried Jude in alarm, tugging at his sleeve.

"I'm afraid I must", he replied softly. He did not explain that he did not want to be seen by the constabulary. Before the girls had time to thank him, he had hurried away.

Unable to make a move of their own volition, the girls helplessly watched him go as the ambulance and a police car arrived together. It was decided that the girls were fit to go home and not long afterwards they were each being comforted by their parents.

Mentally, the police thought that there were several puzzling elements to this case, not least where the rescuers were concerned. They made their notes and settled at the station to await the next emergency call that frequented most Saturday evenings.

Night descended slowly, bringing a cool crispness to the air. The park gates clanged shut. The Keeper went home. The grounds men drifted into nearby pubs, their concern over the frequency of attacks in the park, diminishing as the alcohol took its effect. It would return the following day and that was soon enough.

CHAPTER THREE

A mile away from the park, four shocked and angry handcuffed youths were being hustled from the back of a van into an empty building by the two men wearing dark glasses, and a large Alsatian dog. The building was on a quiet street, had a drive-in entrance, a large underground set of rooms and an overgrown area to the rear.

The youths made token signs of resistance, quickly squashed by growls from the dog and the sight of bulky gun-shaped shapes under the men's jackets. Every few yards, the column would stop and one youth at a time would be propelled into one of the small, almost bare rooms, each door being firmly locked behind them.

Inside each room was a narrow bed, a chair, a bucket and strangely, a loudspeaker mounted high up out of reach and connected to a remote tape recorder.

Each youth reacted somewhat differently. One slouched onto the floor, tears streaming down his face as he wondered why he had been brought there and what was going to happen to him.

The second youth assumed there would be a hidden camera focussed on him and with a show of defiant bravado, lay down on the bed, hands beneath his head, smirking as if he were not a tiny bit apprehensive.

The third youth was the smallest, and wiry. His face was pale and he was unable to hide his shaking. He sat on the chair, tightly gripping the edge of the seat and nervously rocked himself back and forth.

Meanwhile, their appointed leader was pacing up and down inside his cell-like room, muttering to himself and cursing. Every now and then, he would kick at the door and mouth obscenities to the people outside, but they had left the youths alone for the night, to brood over this new turn of events. The tape recorders too, remained silent. Nor could the lads converse, because the walls were solid brick. They could not take comfort from their nearness to one another.

By contrast, Patti and Jude, cocooned in their comforting family circles, were beginning to recover from their ordeal. In a strange, unaccountable way, they were beginning to revel in telling their tale. Jude's father was thankful that his daughter was not a year or two older. She had not yet reached the highly emotive stage of being a teenager and by the way she was able to talk so freely about her experience now, he thought the mental effect might prove to be minimal.

Trying to hide his anger, stronger because it was impotent, he was frustrated knowing that he would probably not be able to discover who the thugs were. So he turned his attention to her rescuers.

"What did he look like? Tell me everything you can remember about him, Jude. For instance, was he wearing a ring? Did he speak with an accent? Was he tall or short?" and so the questions went on.

"I honestly can't remember much about the man who comforted us and we never saw the others."

Inspector Rees-Jones had advised both sets of parents that the girls would possibly recall more details after a day or two, when the shock had begun to subside, but Clifford Barrow could not blot out the picture of his daughter's distress or her tear stained face when the police had brought her home. He needed action. He not only wanted to thank her saviour most sincerely, but he hoped that the man would be able to help identify who the attackers were. The louts had behaved abominably and deserved to be punished and he, for one, was ready and willing to do just that.

Jude did not admit that she had been too ashamed to look into the man's face.

"He did have a very deep voice, soft and reassuring," she offered and with that he had to be content.

Jude's mother Carol came in with a tray of drinks. There were three cups of tea poured out, but she did not touch hers. She was filled with horror and revulsion, not only because of what had happened, but more perhaps because of what could have followed. She felt as if she would never be able to let her daughter out of her sight again.

Clifford looked across at his wife with understanding and concern. Parents are so vulnerable, he thought. He went over and sat on the arm of her chair, his own arm protectively around her. He would have to be the strong one for all the family. Somehow, he would hide his own distress to ensure that Carol did not go to pieces. He must not allow her to become neurotic over this incident, not to the extent that their lives would be ruined anyway.

Slowly, the family settled into a more comfortable normality, so that when Jude eventually fell into a deep sleep, her father heaved her up into his arms and carried her upstairs, careful not to awaken her younger brother Gary, in the next bedroom. They had all agreed to keep the assault details from him, to Jude's obvious relief.

Meanwhile, much the same was taking place in Patti's house nearby and both sets of parents were up long after their families had gone to bed.

CHAPTER FOUR

Night engulfed the town. Thin silver moonbeams penetrated the odd square and alley. Occasionally, it picked out a skulking figure, including one shivering sixteen year old, who stealthily let himself in through the back door of his house, going straight up to his bedroom without calling out to let his parents know he was home.

Elsewhere, other families were beginning to feel ill at ease. In Brook Street, not far from where the returning youth lay shivering, a light still glowed downstairs in a shabby villa that should have been demolished years ago. Elsie Evans kept glancing at the clock on the mantelpiece. Her son Carl had apparently promised to take a new girlfriend to the Tower Disco and the girl, Sheila had come to confront him for standing her up. She sat opposite Elsie, her badly applied make-up creasing as she frowned and sat mostly in sullen silence. Eventually, she decided that he was unlikely to be taking her anywhere that night and with barely a civil *ta-ra*, she showed herself out.

"I'll make sure he calls round to apologise, tomorrow," Elsie promised.

"You needn't bother," the girl flung back at her impolitely. Then she had clattered away on her high heels across the dingy pavement and was lost to the night.

Two doors away from Carl's house, at number six, Maisie Edwards was listening out for the sound of her son coming home.

"Is that you Benny?" she called out as she heard the front door slam.

"No, it's me," slurred her husband Lewis. It will be two o'clock in the morning before that young rascal comes creeping in," he affirmed.

"Yes, but he and the lads were going to the Tower Ballroom tonight, to a disco and he wouldn't go there in his old khaki togs." Her voice had taken on a now too familiar whine, which her husband recognised with distaste.

"Come to bed, woman. He'll come home when he chooses and not before, so stop your caterwauling. He's not a child any longer."

Maisie knew better than to cross her husband when he had had a few beers, so she obediently followed him upstairs, but left the light on in a small act of defiance.

Not far away, in the next block of narrow houses, two other mothers reacted to their sons' non-appearances quite differently. If the truth were known, one of them was glad she didn't have a recalcitrant teenager to deal with, demanding a clean shirt again for the disco, which she hadn't yet bothered to iron. The only concern both these mums had was whether their sons had got into trouble with the police again and whether they would have to be hauled out of their armchairs to go down to the police station to see what charges were being brought. Neither was bothered enough though to stop watching television and their concerns were fleeting.

As the days passed and four youths had still not returned home, their families were at best anxious and at worst puzzled or annoyed. Also, what was even more strange, none of their usual friends had come round asking for them. Eventually, Maisie and Elsie got together and decided to report their sons missing. For the last few days, they had left their doors on the latch and their sleeping had become intermittent and shallow. But the only visitor that had crept up their stairs was Unease.

Across the town, where the houses were slightly larger and well-kept, a man walked home with his dog. It was three in the morning and he let himself into the house, quietly going immediately upstairs. Behind him, Max trotted silently after a long gulp of water from his dish in the kitchen. The man entered the bathroom and ran the water as quietly as he could, so as not to wake up his wife.

His hands were bruised and the skin over one knuckle was torn to reveal an angry looking red blister. He took a jar of ointment out of the cupboard and rubbed it onto his skin. Then his eyes gleamed in the darkness as he bent to pat his best friend

"Goodnight, Max," he whispered. "You have done well." He entered the bedroom and softly closed the door, leaving Max on guard on the landing. Soon both were fast asleep.

Next day, Maisie and Elsie arrived at the police station where the sergeant took their particulars and sent the women away with some hope, as he had no reference of them being in trouble. He suggested that they may have gone on an impulsive jaunt and would come home when they were ready.

When the women had gone away, he settled in the canteen with his mates for a welcome lunch. Casually his detective friends asked him if he had heard anything interesting and he told them of the two mothers and their names.

"Well," grinned Detective Ossie Davies to his friend Bob, "now we know the names of two of them. That should frighten them further." Just then, their detective friend Gwyn Jones came up to the table and signalled them to leave the canteen through the kitchen door. As he ushered them out quickly, they wondered what the urgency was.

"I have just seen young Jude and her father at the registration desk," he whispered. "We should clear out until they leave."

All three hurried out through the door, when Bob remembered he had left his dog in the reception area and ran back into the building. Inside, he called Max softly, but the young girl turned at the sound of his voice. Quickly, he smiled and put a silencing finger to his lips. Jude understood that he did not want to be recognised. She was thrilled to think that she knew his secret, and hoped she wouldn't be tempted to tell anyone. She would try and keep it to herself.

CHAPTER FIVE

Less than three hundred yards from where the dog and his master slept, a tape recorder began to whirr, softly at first, then at a moderate volume. The four thugs found it impossible to escape from the deep voice that intoned from the tape. Each small room was filled with words being drummed mercilessly into them.

Occasionally there would be a pause, but before hopes could be raised it would continue with its clear, but unwelcome message.

"Love one another.

Hurting someone hurts yourself.

Doing your worst will destroy you, not others.
Enjoy your life by letting others enjoy theirs."

Over and over again the tape rolled on, repeating its message relentlessly. A few hours later, it stopped to let them get some rest and hopefully to let them ponder. By morning, each of the young men had slept for very short fitful spells and awoke feeling groggy and anxious.

Someone with a face hidden behind a mask now, let one out. Somehow the watchers had discovered his name was Carl and he was startled when the masked man used his name. That the man knew his identity, sent something approaching terror into Carl's already unsettled mind. To his amazement, he was led outside into a large, overgrown garden. The Alsatian he had seen in the park was squatting nearby eyeing him. He was given a spade and told to dig.

Carl feared that he was being asked to dig his own grave but the man gave no sign, but just ordered him to dig.

The ground was hard and Carl was unused to hard work. Soon, he was out of breath and feeling exhausted, but whenever he tried to stop, the dog would snarl, so he toiled on. An hour went by before he was allowed to stop. Just as he was preparing to swing the spade at his captor, it was roughly taken from him by a previously unseen man. Then, he was led back into his cell.

The procedure was repeated for each youth. When Benny heard the man use his name he had the same reaction as Carl. Each of the thugs became weary very quickly as they dug, their faces resentful and surly.

Across the town at St. John's Vicarage, the minister would have been astounded if he had known his young son Trevor had taped one of his sermons. He would have been even more surprised to learn it had been taped for the choirmaster, who in turn had given it to his son Bob. But neither Trevor, his dad, or the choirmaster could have guessed how and where it was being played. As it was, each day continued much the same for the captives. Strangely, by now, they were beginning to enjoy the gardening as the digging was replaced by planting and at least one of them was beginning to show pleasure as he saw the garden taking on a new shape and realised that he had been part of its transformation.

So the monotonous days went on, relieved only by the garden work. A week had passed since the incident in the park and now unsurprisingly, the cells were needed for new residents. Suddenly, the four friends were jostled into the back of the same van that had transported them from the park, driven to an isolated location and released.

They appeared crestfallen and subdued but Bob wasn't convinced that would last. He just hoped they had learnt some lesson, however shallow.

"You are free to go," he told them sternly. "I doubt if any of the messages on the tape have got through your thick skulls, but I am telling you now, we shall be watching you and your so-called friends. You will never know whether or not we are near you, but should we find you ever attacking young girls or anyone else again, you will be brought back here sharpish and you won't have it so easy next time."

With that admonishment, they youths hustled away into the evening dusk, and to mixed reactions, returned to their homes.

It would be good to end this story with talk of an Utopian town springing up out of the slums, with much reduced crime and violence. It would be good to say that the park thereafter was safe for all ages to enjoy.

All that can be said, is that the watchers continued to try their best, that one or maybe two thugs changed their ways for the better and that one young woman grew up to be a dedicated policewoman. Who knows, she may yet join the watchers.

WHAT WE START,
SOMEONE ELSE
MAY FINISH

ONE

Madeleine sighed. Ahead of her yawned another predictable day of heavy dullness, unless for once she could summon up the courage to do something positive about her life. Already she felt the all too familiar lethargy seep into her. She felt depressed and unable to shake off the languor and as she made vague attempts at tidying up the sitting room, she was conscious that she had lost the ability to play a part. For years she had made housework tolerable by pretending she was on stage; the maid in a smart modern detached house uptown, an au pair, planted by MI5 in a house where the master was suspected to be a spy working for the Russians; the house-keeper in a sprawling mansion set in its own grounds, poor in circumstances beforehand, and now working against clock for fear of losing her position and a roof over her head. Her list of parts had seemed unending, but now the years of daydreaming were beginning to lose their cushioning effect. It would have to be today.

There was to be no further deliberation, no more nights spent in a nightmarish whirl of incoherent thought and half determinations. Today her disillusionment could still give room for positive action. Tomorrow she would have begun the decline into acceptance.

The doorbell rang. She crossed the room with a little more of her natural vigour and entered the hall. Through the glass door she could see the outline of two dark heads. She would put it to them today. She opened the door and gave a welcoming smile.

"Sorry we're late." Jay pushed past her and sank into a deep armchair without further preamble. She stripped off her woolly hat and long garishly striped scarf and dropped them both onto the carpet in an untidy heap. Madeleine smiled. Jay was so comfortable to be with. Neither of them were domesticated by inclination. It was so relaxing to be with someone who would settle for tea in a mug. Fair play for Chrissie, too. Although of the three, she was much the tidiest, and methodical in everything she tackled, she was heartwarmingly tolerant and indeed welcomed the difference in true French spirit. She was still struggling out of her boots in the hall, as impolitely deserted by Madeleine as by her fellow visitor. Jay was already puffing away at a cigarette whilst Madeleine was silently shaping her decision to speak into coherent thought.

"Cheer us up, Maddy," cried Chrissie as she at last entered the room, her boots tidied away in the hall cupboard and her duffle hung precariously at the edge of an already bulging hook in the same cupboard. She curled up on the settee.

"God, isn't life boring!"

Jay and Madeleine sighed their agreement.

"You should have gone away, Chrissie. You needed the break."

"There is only one thing worse than being bored–" replied Chrissie, ruffling dark curls that had been flattened beneath her duffle hood.

"And that's being bored on holiday," Jay and Madeleine finished the sentence for her.

Madeleine sensed that this was the moment.

"There is of course no need for us to be bored at all," she said in an effort to keep her voice controlled, lest she betray the excitement now welling up inside her. "There is so much we could do."

"You're not going to suggest we go to pottery classes at the Centre are you?" asked Chrissie with a groan. Madeleine brushed the interruption aside, eager now to put the proposition to them as quickly as possible, lest her courage fail her.

"We could do something exciting, a little dangerous even." She paused for a moment for her words to take effect.

"Yes," scoffed Chrissie. "We have ten days holiday left, or at least I have. You teachers still have a month to go. What dangerous adventure do you suggest we embark upon? A shop trip? Crossing over Corporation Street is becoming more hazardous every day, I suppose."

Jay said nothing. Madeleine was in a strange but deadly serious mood, she could tell. She waited for her friend to continue.

"Right first time," Madeleine went on earnestly. "Yet a trip might not be the best description. 'Lift' is the operative word, I would think!"

Madeleine paused to allow her words to take effect, nervously prepared to laugh it away as a joke and yet sensing again that her timing could not have been better. Both her friends were going through tedious, if not obviously unhappy phases. Jay, a widow of two years, suffered the daily interference of a domineering, self-righteous mother-in-law, who unfortunately lived just across the street from her, in a quiet cul-de-sac. Her own comfortably sized semi-detached had been a present from her father-in-law, Leonard Langton, on her marriage to his son Bill. Jay had had no choice given her. Bill's parents had idolised their son, and it was significant that they had chosen to donate a house practically on their own doorstep. Bill and Jay had been too relieved and delighted to have a house given them, so soon after their student days, that it was not until later that they wished they had insisted on waiting until they could afford the deposit on a house of their own choice. Once accepted, the gift hung over them as a constant reminder of the gratitude they were clearly expected to express almost daily. Bill's untimely accident had come just as they were preparing to risk permanently off-ending the Langtons, by moving elsewhere. Since the accident, Jay had been at first too numb, and later too browbeaten by their constant surveillance to carry the move through. Lately a little more aggression was surfacing as her privacy was being threatened even more and her social life organized by her in-laws to the point of almost being taken over. Without the interest and demands of her Deputy Headship at the local school, she would have been completely subdued by such consistent dominance. During the last six months her own personality was rebelliously coming more and more to into force. Her sincere, unaffected approach to life made the social climbing and false standards of her in-laws' narrow world more and more intolerable and now that Bill's memory was less painful for her, she was beginning to see that she must assert herself.

Chrissie too had problems. When she had married Jim, he had been quiet but interesting. He could, it seemed, talk about any subject, serious or jocular. He had been such a stimulating companion; Chrissie had not hesitated when he proposed. He had made her feel an intelligent companion, with contributions worth listening to. After ten years of marriage, unfortunately, the stream of words had ceased to flow between them. It was as if he had wooed her with words, and then having won her, had left them to hang silently in his own brain, as he sat and pondered over world events in silent contemplation. Chrissie, however, had been awakened by his ardent verbalism. After their marriage, she had become a part-time social worker. Her colleagues were very much as her husband had been in those far off days. They were lively and stimulating in their case discussions, tackling each new problem with an earnest enthusiasm. So it was that Chrissie found herself living in two different worlds, swinging from

THE COTTAGE OF SECRETS

the hectic inspirations of the mornings, to the almost silent, uncommunicative evenings with her husband. Like Jay and Madeleine, she found the friendship of their trio, a welcome lifeline.

Jay was first to speak.

"For a moment, I thought you meant shoplifting," she giggled rather unconvincingly. At the same time an image of her father-in-law's moustache twitching in outrage as she was being hauled before the judge, flashed before her. It would be almost worth it, just to see that officious gentleman for once at a loss for words. Madeleine brought her back to the present with a jerk.

"I did," she confirmed, taking a deep breath. "I did." She caught a glimpse of Chrissie's mouth forming a wordless 'Oh' and hurried on. "Just for a sort of dare, you know, not to keep anything; just for the fun of pitting our wits against authority, doing something one shouldn't before life becomes so boring we shall accept it as the norm. I mean, just look at us. Another ten years and we'll be middle aged. We'll be sitting here dramatically outpointing each other with our symptoms of the dreaded change. Our best friends will be the chemist and the lady running the knitting shop down the road."

"Never!" cried Jay emphatically. She had never been able to knit any stitch other than plain and had spent most of her life resisting attempts to improve on her lack of skill. All the same, despite her rejection of her friend's perspicacious image, she recognised the despair behind the image and realised that Madeleine was quite possibly in earnest. Without thinking, she carried the idea a stage further.

"We could donate the stolen goods to the poor. I always fancied myself as a female Robin Hood."

"I hadn't thought any further than the deed," confessed Madeleine, "but don't think that I'm not serious, because I am. I'm so tired of being bored. I could go out of my mind sometimes, and now the holidays are here, it's even worse. Two weeks in Austria has done nothing to make me feel more settled. If anything it has unsettled me even further. I must do something and something quick."

Jay and Chrissie heard their friend in silent sympathy. Unlike them, Madeleine had never married. Lively and articulate in the company of her own sex and the children she taught in the same school as Jay, her personality wilted in the presence of men. Brought up by an elderly aunt after her parents had both been killed in the war, she had grown up in a world of women, and women mostly many years her senior. It was easy to understand how she had fallen under the spell of Rowland Evans, who was happily married and blissfully unaware of Madeleine's existence other than as a quiet, unassuming fellow member of staff. The fact that Madeleine longed for the school days to begin, so that she could catch even an occasional glimpse of him on those days, would have astounded him. Jay hoped that he would never know. She wondered how long it would be before other members of staff would become aware of the covert but adoring glances Madeleine cast his way. Madeleine was still speaking.

"We have another month before term begins. Why not, for once, do something different." In her mind, she pictured Rowland comforting her after she had been charged, assuring her that he knew she was innocent. He would fight for her to the bitter end. Her maudlin flight into Victorian melodrama deserted her as her sense of humour brought a smile and the image was erased. Chrissie was shocked. She felt she ought to say something, change the subject even, but nothing came to mind.

Jay, anxious to help Madeleine by pretending to go along with the idea was still making facetious remarks.

"We'll start with the shoe shops. I could do with some new boots. Then there's that new store opened in Harborne. They have rails and rails of super dresses there, and lots of those high necked frilly blouses."

At last Chrissie found her voice.

"I thought we were supposed to be giving them to the poor," she muttered, as if reluctant to be considered an eager participant in this conversation.

"I am poor," laughed Jay, who spent her money as fast as she earned it, much to her in-laws' disgust, and thereby affording them ample opportunity to carp and rant at her.

"Not as poor as some of my clients," sighed Chrissie. She warmed to the theme if not to putting it into practice.

"I'd love to be able to walk into Eaton Street and surprise Mrs. Darby with a new, smart, stylish coat for once. She's only thirty, but she looks almost twice that, what with her frumpy jumble sale clothes, her lank hair and that worn look that never seems to leave her face. Now she's what I call poor."

"Is that the one with four children and another on the way?" asked Madeleine.

"Yes, and I doubt if any of the children share the same father," answered Chrissie solemnly. "I was looking at her the other day, with this new fellow hanging about the place, out of work and sponging off her for beer money, and I couldn't help wondering how one human being could get herself into such a mess, and then of course I kept wondering how it is the rest of us let her."

"Well then." said Madeleine, "Think of the joy you could give her. Why don't we make her our first beneficiary? Her and the children. Why, we could fit them all out for the holiday. Are they going anywhere?"

"The department have fixed them up with a fortnight at the seaside, Barry Island, I think, but we can't take the parents as well. Besides, the only holiday the likes of Mrs. Darby would get, would be to be without the children for a while."

"Right then, it's settled," said Madeleine, pressing on whilst she felt she was gaining ground. "Settled, barring the details," she added.

"Steady on Maddy, you sound as if you really mean it," protested Chrissie.

"She does," confirmed Jay. She lit another cigarette and began to pace the room. "She does mean it. Can't you see?"

Jay knew Madeleine so well but now suddenly she

discovered something about herself. She was neither surprised nor shocked. Chrissie looked from one to the other. Jay, tall and broad-framed with her high wide cheekbones and larqe but attractive mouth. Madeleine, a slim five foot two, blonde and freckled sitting absolutely still. For the first time it hit her that there was a real possibility that something could really come of this chatter. Ruefully she found herself wondering if she was going to give her husband a talking point in his life again. From that small thought leapt another.

"Why not?" she thought. "Why not?" This time she spoke her thoughts aloud. "We could do it, but we should give the goods back. After all, it would be just as awkward to replace them as to take them in the first place."

Madeleine sighed, a deep sigh that seemed to come up from her toes. She had done it. A heady giddiness swept over her and she felt a hot flush spread across her face. Anger followed. If she were going to allow herself to be sick just when talking about it, going any further would be pointless. She pulled herself together and felt her head clear.

"We'll plan it now," she said, and so they did.

TWO

Jay dropped Chrissie off, then drove her Mini expertly through the rush-hour traffic. The journey was short once she had managed to cross the main thoroughfare from the city to the south, and she was soon turning into the cul-de-sac. Her heart sank as she saw the familiar military stride of her father-in-law crossing over towards her house. It was too late to turn back and let him find her out. Even as the thought crossed her mind, he turned and waved, then proceeded to irritate her instantly, by taking it upon himself to direct her in to the garage. Perversely, she stopped the car at the end of the drive. Let him think she was going out. That would give him and mum-in-law something to think about. She was pleased that she had managed to stop without a judder, or that would have brought forth another lecture. Forcing a smile, she gave him a wave and eased out of the car.

"Hello, Dad," she called brightly, then frowned. She had always managed to avoid calling him Dad or Father or indeed anything. Why had she suddenly let that slip? She almost added, "What do you want now?" but restrained herself. The afternoon had refreshed her, armed her a little perhaps with a little more tolerance. Then she thought of her husband Bill, with his honest open face and his good-natured kindness to all he met and she forced another smile. Still part of her resisted and she stood with her key poised over the keyhole as if invited him to state his business and go.

"Well aren't we going in?" he asked imperiously.

"Well, I am in rather a rush," Jay said breathlessly, as if to emphasise the shortness of time. "Did you want something?"

"Not here, lass, not here," he replied gruffly, and so resignedly she turned the key and opened the door.

The house was warm and welcoming, a startling blend of bright oranges, yellows and flame splashes, toned down just a little by soft mint green and wooden wall panelling in a rich toffee brown. The open plan styling accommodated the bold colours and large patterns well, for the main area was long and wide. The whole effect was one of comfort and brightness.

Jay gazed in dismay at the disarray before her. Her father-in-law would not comment himself, but tomorrow there would be remarks from his Floss. She turned quickly, in time to see his eyes slide across the room before withering her with a familiar but thankfully silent criticism.

"What is it?" she asked pointedly, glancing at her watch as if she were about to dash out again without delay.

"Can't I just pop in to see how you are, dear?" Then came the real reason. "You've been gone rather a long time this afternoon. Mother and I were becoming anxious."

Jay did not answer the unspoken question, but hurried into the kitchen to put the kettle on.

"I'm fine," she called. For a while there was an uncomfortable silence, his way of trying to force her to be a little more forthcoming, she knew, but for once she refused to let the silence bother her. Quietly as if he were not there, she made herself a cup of tea and cut a cheese sandwich before returning to the living room, with them balanced in each hand. Her guilt at not having poured one for her father-in-law vanished into anger as she saw him pointedly pick up an ash-tray from the armchair and a magazine from another and then place them carefully on the long pine coffee table. It was clear he intended to sit down, but the swing of the day from tedium to excitement and on to pomposity gave her impatient courage. Deftly she manoeuvred herself so that she stood at an angle to the chair, making it just a little awkward for him to sit there. She managed to set the mug and sandwich down on the chair-arm and then moved towards the door into the hallway, something in her attitude showing clearly that she quite naturally expected him to be behind her. Indeed she talked all the way.

"It was good of you to come over, but I must get on now." To his surprise he found himself at the door, out-manoeuvred for the first time in their relationship. Too thick-skinned normally to be sensitive to a situation, nevertheless some vestige of instinct warned him to go quietly and not to enquire further concerning where she had been that afternoon, or where she planned to go after his departure.

Jay smiled as she watched him depart huffily. She guessed he and Floss would be at their curtains this evening; watching for her to leave the house. Well they would watch in vain. Flinging the magazine across the room in childish defiance, she settled down to enjoy a quiet evening at home, thinking, thinking, thinking.

THREE

Chrissie was also sitting thinking, wondering how she had ever agreed to go ahead with the others and comforting herself over and over again with the thought that tomorrow it would all appear in the outrageously criminal light it was, and that the whole scheme would be forgotten. Still it had been fun planning something a little daring for a change. Better than the usual decisions of what to cook for the evening meal. Tonight they had had plaice in cheese sauce, Jim's favourite. He had thanked her politely. He always thanked her for his meals. She thought as if she had to acknowledge his good points in order to correct her more critical appraisal of him all day. But what had he said since?

"Nothing much in the paper tonight, dear. I'll switch on the television to see the news. Something must have happened somewhere."

"Yes, it did," she thought. "Your wife was planning to become a criminal, aided and abetted if not downright urged on, by her two closest, and I might add, most respectable friends!"

She took up a magazine but found it impossible to concentrate. She took out her workload for the morning but even that failed to hold her interest. She found herself waiting for Jim to speak. She was even timing him.

At 8.15, he coughed.

"It's alright, I've got a frog in my throat, dear."

At 9.23, "How about a cup of tea?" so obediently she went and put the kettle on.

"Want anything to eat, dear?" she called.

"No, thank you," came the reply, followed by another, "thank you," as she put the tea down on a small table beside his chair.

Finally, at 10.30, "I think it's time to lock up," and a ,"Good-night dear, I think I'll go up now," and he was gone. Little more than two score words all evening she thought. She thought back to the first night she had met him. She had made some tactless ill-informed comment on the Mau-Mau risings in Kenya although there had been peace in that area for several years. Jim had astounded her with his background knowledge and insight into the problems. He had been able to identify with both the rebels and with the white settlers. Later, he was to demonstrate the same informed knowledge of world affairs and their evenings became a source of delight for Chrissie. She had fallen in love with his rhetoric, and at the time, the unvaried and unimaginative settings where they met went unnoticed. Looking back now, she realised that they had almost unfailingly met at the same pub, drunk the same drinks and parted with the same rather passionless embraces. She had been mesmerised, not so much by his mind, but by the doors opening within her own. She suddenly found that she too could reason out, could think and make intelligent or at least reasoned conclusions. It was as if she were a late developer and was now ready and eager to learn.

Three months later they were married. The world still offered its daily excitements in the foreign news columns or home affairs. Only the need for Jim to 'educate' her seemed to have evaporated. To her dismay, she realised he had needed the audience of the pub customers as much as he had needed her. Whilst she had been listening with rapt attention, he had been perhaps sub-consciously playing to the crowd. At home, the audience reduced to one, his interest had diminished to nil.

Outside, the traffic drones grew less frequent, lights were dimmed at house after house, and the silence of the early hours prevailed. Still Chrissie made no move to go to bed. Her mind was churning over the past and the present until finally it steadied itself to mull over Madeleine's strange proposition. When at last she eased herself into the bed beside Jim's slumbering figure, a last thought came to her through her drowsy brain.

"If Madeleine were in earnest, well I guess I will go along with it too, just for the hell of it; only we'll have to give it all back the very next day." Within minutes she was fast asleep.

***

Madeleine had hardly slept at all. Excitement and nervousness kept her jerking back to consciousness just as she seemed to be falling asleep at last. At five o'clock she could stand it no longer. She dressed and washed and went downstairs to make a cup of tea. She wondered whether to make it a herbal cup but she could not remember which one was likely to have a sedative effect and the labels told her nothing. I must get myself a book on herbs, she thought, then with a wry smile it crossed her mind that perhaps she could pinch one!

Abruptly that thought jerked her wide awake. The excitement of the planning had been always the predominant thought before but she had always been dimly aware that the whole 'adventure,' for want of a better word, could easily get out of hand. They might enjoy the escapade too much, but Madeleine had enough sense left to be fully aware of the foolishness of repeating the deed.

"We will do it once after careful planning. Then we will return whatever we manage to take with equal care. That should be as much fun as removing something, and then perhaps we'll have something to talk about. It will spur us on to other more legitimate and exciting ventures, I'm sure."

She realised she was trying to justify the situation. It was true that she felt guilty now, especially as it had been entirely her idea. That the other two would fall in with her plans she was absolutely sure. She settled for a cup of ginseng tea to clear her brain and keep her resolve.

Jay and Chrissie arrived at ten. It was soon apparent that all three had been thinking along the same lines. Each emphasised that anything taken would be given back secretly but swiftly the following day, that this would be their one and only attempt at breaking the law, and Chrissie led them onto a third idea.

"There is no way we can keep any of the garments,

always supposing we can successfully remove them," she uttered seriously, sidestepping the word stealing. "But it would be nice if we clubbed together and bought some things for the Darby's. I mean we could be legitimately buying Mrs. Darby a coat, and the kids some items of clothing, small ones I mean, whilst trying to outwit the salespeople at the same time."

"But that would mean taking things from more than one store," protested Jay. "I thought we had agreed we should visit one shop and one shop only. We mustn't let this get this out of hand. I want to return to my job in September, not spend my days sitting them out in a grey cell in some bleak prison somewhere out in wilds."

Madeleine saw that they would as swiftly talk themselves out of the jaunt if she didn't bring the conversation round to more positive thinking.

"We'll go to a store that caters for adults and children. You and I will go back to school as normal in September, Chrissie will not become a customer for her Probation Officer friends, and you can keep your coats on," she added, as Jay began to disrobe, "because we are going out now to have a look at Selby's and see what we can work out. With a little luck, we might be able to get it over with this morning."

Chrissie glanced nervously at the other two but she followed them to the car without protest. During the short journey, each was silent yet perhaps not surprisingly for three respectable people who had never knowingly broken the law or thought of it before, their thoughts were channelled along similar lines. Each was silently showing withdrawal signs. Jay was quietly determined that they would go ahead with the fun of planning it all out, but when the moment came, none of them would have the nerve to carry it through. Relieved by this comforting train of thought she drove carefully and smoothly through the morning traffic. Chrissie too had decided the joke would soon end and concentrated her thoughts on thinking what they could get for Mrs. Darby and her family and how they could present them without Mrs. Darby knowing they had been especially bought.

"We could say they had been claimed from the unredeemed luggage department at the railway station," she mused. "But then perhaps Mrs. Darby would realise its possibilities and start hounding the railway officials at the Goods Department." Her mind steadied itself along lines of similar thought, so that when Jay entered the car park at the rear of Selby's Store, she was brought back to reality with an unpleasant jolt.

Madeleine did not need to be told of the decisions the others had made. She knew she too was wavering and the other two were entering the store too happily despite their obvious nerves.

"Well, we can still have the fun of planning it," was the thought that crossed her mind as they crossed the threshold and entered the Ladies Wear Department.

The department was long and narrow. Bored looking assistants stood at intervals. There were no counters for them to pretend to tidy and apart from Madeleine and Co. there were no customers. Jay sighed with relief. Now she could say openly what she had been thinking.

"We'd better just stick to planning something without accomplishing the deed," she said firmly. "The recession is hitting all the stores. We are the only customers and the spotlight would be on us all the time." To her further relief, the others nodded their agreement. They began to relax.

"Let's look for a coat for Mrs. Darby," suggested Chrissie.

"Hey, don't lets abandon everything," protested Madeleine. "Let's at least go ahead with the thinking."

"Well come and pretend to be looking at these imitation fur coats," whispered Jay. "We are beginning to attract attention."

They moved towards the coats and began to finger them idly.

"This time of day is out for a start," said Madeleine. "Lunch time would be best. The office workers will be filling in their lunch hour and some of these assistants will be on their lunch break, so there will be less vigilance."

The coats were beautiful and of a quality not usually shown at this store. An assistant moved over towards them.

"Lovely, aren't they?" she purred, getting ready to go into her sales talk patter. "Actually, they are on loan from another branch. We are trying them out. Luckily –" she added encouragingly, "we have the right clientele and they are selling very well. If you like this one madam, I should snap it up. Another customer was very interested yesterday and intimated that she would return with her husband this morning."

"Go on, try it on," urged Jay, feeling uncomfortable with the assistant so pressingly near.

"Alright, I will," agreed Madeline, knowing that at over one hundred pounds it was priced well out of her reach. She followed the hopeful assistant into a booth and placed her bag upon a chair. Jay edged in, in such a way as to edge the assistant out.

"I'm becoming expert at manoeuvring people," she smiled to herself, remembering her father-in-law the evening before. She turned her back deliberately and after a moment's hovering, the assistant moved away.

Madeleine sighed. The coat, was beautiful, but she was too short to carry its bulk elegantly.

"I look like Grandma Giles," she thought ruefully. "You try it, Jay."

Jay put her bag beside Madeleine's.

"I'm broader than you across the shoulder," she demurred. "It won't fit me." Nevertheless, she slipped into the coat. She was right. It pulled across the shoulders and was uncomfortably tight.

"You need the next size, Madam." The assistant had appeared from nowhere and held another similar coat over her arm. Jay had little option but to comply. This time it fitted beautifully.

Jay's added height and dark auburn hair were enhanced by the russet dyes of the fibres, complimenting the coat in a way Madeleine's fair and shorter image could not. She turned and pirouetted before the long mirror. Madeleine began to feel concern. Jay was notoriously careless with her money. If they stayed here much longer

Jay would buy it and run up another giant overdraft with her all too accommodating bank.

"Before you spend all that money, you ought to think about it," she said, looking at Jay meaningfully. "Why not sleep on it? We could come in again tomorrow and have a fresh look at it then."

"Well, of course Madam must do as she sees fit," interrupted the assistant, her middle aged face crinkling into well marked frown lines, "but I should warn you that we are not expecting any more in for quite a while. Perhaps Madam should have a few minutes to think about it. It looks absolutely you, if I may say so," she added, holding her ground and making no move to leave them alone.

Jay knew Madeleine was right. Ever impulsive she had been quite prepared to buy the coat. Now she paused, wondering if Madeleine was thinking of their planning venture when she had proposed returning tomorrow. Madeleine gave her another meaning look and she obediently took her cue and handed the coat back.

"I'll probably be back tomorrow," she said with a broad smile, in an attempt to cheer up the assistant, who now stood with lips pursed in a superior, disapproving pucker, which served only to emphasise the large mole above her lip.

"Very well, Madam. The choice is of course yours."

FOUR

Chrissie was waiting impatiently by the racks of Separates, obviously impatient to be gone. During her wait, her eye had been taken by the suede waistcoats and Mrs. Darby's new wardrobe had been pushed to the back of her mind it seemed, for she turned towards the exit, as her friends approached.

"What's the rush?" asked Jay. "We are supposed to be picking up ideas, and what happened to the worthy Mrs. Darby's need of a smart new coat?"

"Yes, hold your horses, Chrissie," enjoined Madeleine, as Chrissie began heading determinedly towards the door. Chrissie slowed and turned back reluctantly to rejoin them.

"The cheaper coats are over to the right," she muttered and led the way to a long rack of coats placed along the wall. "We mustn't get a very expensive one," she advised, "or Mrs. Darby will be afraid to wear it. She'll probably hang it in the wardrobe for best and it would be seen only at funerals. She might start wondering about its origin too," she added, still determined that Mrs. Darby should think the coat had been somehow passed on. Chrissie knew how galling it must be for someone to be in a consistently humble position, always having to be grateful, especially at the hands of the self-righteous do-gooder. She felt it was essential that the gift should not appear as a gift at all but as an unwanted garment simply and unceremoniously passed on. Accepting gifts for the children was more natural and would not go against the grain so much, she felt sure.

"A middle-of-the-road coat would be best," agreed Jay and she indicated a rack near the window. Together all three moved to the rack, Madeleine and Jay standing slightly back to allow Chrissie to make the choice. Neither of them had knowingly set eyes on Mrs. Darby, although they had heard a great deal about her and her largely self-induced troubles.

To their surprise, Chrissie made no more than a cursory review of the coats, and almost immediately picked out a simple coat in bottle green velour, with a small grey mock fur collar.

Madeleine had been thinking how strange it was to see autumn and winter clothes on sale so early, but she knew it was not unusual and this month was typical of the wet and windy Augusts they had been having lately. Now she glanced in distaste at the bottle green monstrosity before her. Jay voiced her thoughts for her.

"Whatever happened to our banner-waving social worker, dedicated to the cause of the poor downtrodden?" she asked in mock amazement. "I thought we were going to get Mrs. Darby something special, not this old fashioned apology for style. What's the matter with you, Chrissie? Put it back and choose something that will give your Mrs. Darby some pleasure to receive." She took the coat away from Chrissie and replaced it on the rack.

"Chrissie's still nervous," thought Madeleine, whose own nerves had settled now that she had come to her senses and acknowledged the madness of her anti-boredom scheme.

Chrissie turned shamefacedly towards the rack and began to rummage through the assorted styles again.

"You're right, of course," she muttered glumly and with a nervous sigh. "I keep thinking I should be doing my visits. I mustn't delay them for too long or there will be a pile of complaints on my desk in the morning. We should have kept this episode for the afternoon as we agreed."

"Well, you're late anyway, so the degree of lateness won't alter things greatly," said Madeleine gently. "That's a nice one," she added, as Chrissie held up a bright Cherry red coat with a stylish mandarin collar. Then as Chrissie still looked tense, she went on, "besides you are always putting in over-time and unpaid at that."

"In my job, it's impossible not to," sighed Chrissie, holding up the coat to give it a more critical appraisal. "This one is much better, don't you think?" Jay and Madeleine nodded their agreement and Chrissie handed it over to a puzzled young assistant who emerged form the background.

"But this is not your size, Madam. Wouldn't you care to try one on first? I'm sure we have one in your size. Let me see, at a guess I should say Madam is a size ten." She paused to allow the not so subtle flattery to take effect.

"Size twelve actually," replied Chrissie shortly. "This is not for me. It is for–" she meant to say "a friend," but changed it swiftly to, "my mother."

As the assistant walked away, her young face

beaming understanding, Madeleine and Jay exchanged knowing glances, silently acknowledging to each other that Chrissie was behaving oddly. She appeared strung-up.

"We'll go and sort something out for the kids," said Jay, "whilst you settle up here. Stay here and relax. We're not going to do anything," she went on comfortingly. "We never really were, you chump. Calm down."

"I can't relax and I can't calm down," cried Chrissie in an urgent whisper, emphasising the first person dramatically. "I've already done it!"

"Done what?" asked Madeleine in a carbon copy whisper, rejecting at first the thought that first pushed its way into her brain but then as she saw her friend's eyes looking frantically from one to the other, the suspicion took firm hold.

"Done what?" echoed Jay suspecting the worst.

Chrissie was too choked to reply. Instead she fumbled with the buttons of her coat, unfastening it at length to show a smart new suede waistcoat, its label still dangling from its top button, set over her plain green dress. Her friends were speechless, and remained so as she refastened the coat.

"Thank God for a cold August," she said in a vain attempt to lighten the moment.

"Chrissie, you're mad," hissed Jay, no less shocked than Chrissie herself. "What made you do it? How did you do it?"

Chrissie struggled to speak, but the words were slow to come. She looked over her shoulder where the young assistant was carefully folding the coat into a large carrier bag, and at last the words came rushing out.

"Everyone started looking at you, when you went into the booth. I think they were all jealously wondering if that assistant was going to make a big sale. Then a few customers drifted in, including the son of one of the assistants who looked as if he was on the borrow. So I grabbed hold of the youngest, least experienced looking assistant I could see. She left me with four jackets to try and I returned three when I could see she was temporarily engaged elsewhere."

Despite the horror at what she had done, Chrissie couldn't help allowing a note of triumph creep into her voice, but there was little pleasure in it.

"And don't ask me why I did it because I don't know. One minute I was idly thinking how something would be taken, and the next I knew, I had done it."

Madeleine was unable to say a word. She was bathed in guilt, she was the prime mover in this stupid affair, she was the instigator of it all and what had she achieved? She had turned one of her closest friends into a thief. Jay too was silent, her mind desperately trying to be busy with rectifying plans but succeeding only in being busy. Chrissie had not finished.

"It's your turns now," she insisted. "After all, that was the original agreement wasn't it? We said we would each take something, not just one of us." Frantic now, she was conveniently pushing aside this morning's retractions.

Jay found her voice.

"I'm not taking a thing," she asserted indignantly. She was terrified and already beginning to shake.

"Neither am I," said Madeleine, her whisper calm, as she made an effort to pull herself together. All this was her fault and she felt it was up to her to keep a clear head if they were to come out of the episode unscathed. Briefly she thought of Rowland. If only she could be so calm where he was concerned. Then Madeleine was given a respite, as the assistant returned with the bag and receipt.

Not wanting to attract further attention, they moved away toward the children's wear. Here they nervously purchased four tee-shirts of varying sizes.

"These are for a friend's children," said Madeleine. "Will she be able to change any of them if they are the wrong size?"

"Provided they are returned to the store within a week, Madam," replied the saleswoman pleasantly. Madeleine began to say her thanks but a signal from the floor manager attracted the woman's attention, and from the pleased expression that flitted across her face, it appeared to be time for her coffee break. She disappeared through a side door.

Madeleine felt quite composed now.

"We must put it back," she said quietly. "We must put it back now."

Jay nodded her agreement.

"Come on, we'll go and try some on. We might even buy one," she added, trying to force a bantering grin as she glanced at Chrissie's white face.

"It's no use. I couldn't go near that booth again. We'll have to get out of here. It won't be long before they discover one waistcoat is missing. They are quite up-to-date on checking their stock these days."

The others knew Chrissie was not speaking blindly. Her work brought her into contact with many people who lived on the fringe of the law. She knew that the stores had tightened their security in many ways. Her choice of an inexperienced young sales-girl, probably just beginning her first job, had been essential to her success. She knew that nowadays, only two garments were allowed to be taken into a booth at a time. In fact, there were discreet notices to that effect, spaced around the store. There was little doubt in her mind that the theft would be very shortly discovered. She felt paralysed with fear and was terrified that her legs would refuse to carry her from the store.

"Now listen, Chrissie. You will come back to the fitting room with us," said Madeleine. "Jay will ask to try on the imitation fur coat again and I–" she paused, then repeated, "I will ask if I can try on some suede waistcoats. The store is filling up. I'll ask the assistant if you can come into the fitting room so that you can see Jay and me, and I'll get into the next booth. You go in with Jay, slip off the waistcoat, pass it to me. I will put it on the chair in my booth, cover it with my coat and return it with the other suede waistcoats later."

Madeleine felt her head wonderfully clear. Taking Chrissie firmly by the arm and giving a bemused Jay a sharp push, they headed towards the area displaying the more expensive coats.

The same assistant came forward eagerly to greet

them, her welcoming smile growing wider as Jay asked to try on the coat again. To give Madeleine more time, Jay asked if she could try-on a jacket at the same time. No sooner had the assistant moved away than Chrissie, spurred on into action now by a ray of hope, slipped into Jay's booth and whilst her friend shielded her, slipped out of the waistcoat and passed it to Madeleine, hovering anxiously outside. Madeleine slipped off her own coat and placed it over the waistcoat. Then she turned towards the surprised assistant.

"Don't raise your hopes," she smiled charmingly. "I'm not thinking of having one as well." Nice touch that, she thought. It implied that Jay was about to make a purchase and would make the saleswoman more amenable surely. "I'd like to try one or two of those suede waistcoats over there, but I'd like to stay near my friend to help her decide which to have." There it was again, the hint of a sale.

The assistant hesitated for a moment and then smiled accommodatingly.

"Strictly speaking, you should use a booth nearer the racks, but I'm sure no one will mind if I bring some waistcoats over here for you."

As the girl approached with the waistcoats over her arm, she entered the booth and made as if to hang them up.

"I'll have them up there," smiled Madeleine firmly. "They are so easily spoiled if not looked after correctly."

To her delight, the girl smiled and hung three waistcoats up on the single hook in the corner. Seeing that she intended to stay and watch, Madeleine tried two of them on quickly. Idly, as she saw the girl watching intently, she asked if there were any darker shades available. At last the girl went off to look. Quickly, her fingers hot and slippery with perspiration, Madeleine picked up the stolen waistcoat.

"Damn," she whistled through her teeth soundlessly. There was no hanger. She had no choice but to slip it onto the third hanger. When the girl returned Madeleine was still viewing the second waistcoat, pretending to be seriously considering it.

"Thank you," she smiled, as the girl handed over a dark green fringed affair, "but I don't think green would be suitable; although I still have one more to try."

Madeline turned and then made a small sound of surprise.

"Oh, there are two waistcoats on this hanger."

"You must have put it on by mistake, Madam," suggested the girl, then stopped as she saw all three hangers were used. She looked around in puzzlement. She was convinced each hanger had had only one waistcoat each when she had brought them in. Still, as long as it wasn't one less. She shrugged her shoulders and watched again as Madeleine tried the third waistcoat on, somehow intuitively knowing that Madeleine's interest was not full-hearted enough to guarantee a sale. She was becoming more interested in the sounds coming from the next booth. So too was Madeleine, who was having a distinctly uneasy feeling that Jay was about to make a purchase. Politely she expressed her regret to the girl and watched with a huge shuddering sigh of relief as the girl took all the waistcoats including the stolen one, back to the racks. Then she picked up her bag, her coat still only half on, and went to give the all clear.

"You're too late. I've bought it," chuckled Jay, her wide smile at its broadest and the saleswoman hurried away as if aware that Madeleine might change her friend's mind. Madeleine was too relieved to have returned the offending article to make any great protest. Deep down, she knew Jay was trying to make Chrissie feel better. In a complicated but entirely female way, Jay was showing Chrissie that she was prepared to pay for what she wanted. An expensive form of assurance but typical of Jay whose generosity of spirit was one of her most heartwarming qualities. Outside the shop, the friends moved silently towards the car park. Once in the car, they collapsed in a huddle of giggling relief.

"Brilliant. You were brilliant, Maddy," smiled Jay, "but you," and playfully she banged Chrissie's head with a rolled up magazine, "don't you ever scare the daylights out of us like that again."

Jay dropped Madeleine first so that she could have Chrissie's company part of the way home. As Madeleine left the car, she put her head back in through the window.

"Look, I can't go without saying how sorry I am this happened. We're extremely fortunate to have come out of this so easily. What I'm trying to say is, it was all my fault, and if I ever get another hare-brained idea like this into my head, I give you permission to pour a bowl of cold water over me."

"Don't think we won't," said Jay grimly, then with a broad smile, she drove off.

★★★

Outside the store Simon Darby and his hanger-on Scott Philips, grinned at each other. They had been laying new carpets in the store's Ladies Department and now it looked like reaping benefits previously unthought of. Simon had recognised Chrissie as a social worker who had visited his mother and with whom he had argued on one or two occasions.

"We saw her take the waistcoat, and we've got her, right and proper," Simon smirked. "Yes, next time Mrs. High and Mighty comes snooping around our house with her nosey parker social worker interference, she might just have a worried look about her, something on her mind, as they say -"

"Yeah, something like an anonymous letter," sneered Scott delightedly.

"And perhaps a spot of money trouble," added Simon. Purposefully, they too went home.

NOT THIS TIME SAM

The cloud came to an abrupt halt as through the haze before him, Sam could see a towering pair of golden gates emerging. Sam squatted on the cloud patiently enough, although he was feeling rather bewildered and forlorn. The air around him was cool and swirled noisily as though hissing out water to the earth below. At last Sam began to feel annoyed at the delay. He had not come all this way to be ignored.

"'urry it up, can't yer?" he called fretfully through the gates. Peevishly, he peered through the mist to where the dim outline of Saint Peter could be seen scanning through pages of the giant book of fates.

"Samuel Alfred Jones?" Saint Peter was muttering to himself. "Perhaps you have another name, brother?"

"That's all I need," thought Sam in disgust, "a ruddy comic up here of all places. I'd better humour him, anyways, just to be on the safe side." Sam gave Saint Peter a sheepish grim. "Yes, brother, I have. Samuel Aleysieus Alfred Jones is me full monicker, and I thought I could have at least left that mouthful behind me. After all, you've pinched me body, real handsome it was too, and me best suit wot was real worsted. Mind you, I bet Ellie me missus, will put me watch and me tankard in me coffin wiv me, knowing them to be me most treasured possessions – together wiv me Bible, of course," he added hastily. "But where will they go mate?" he pondered, "up in the perishing smoke, I shouldn't wonder, and here I am, dead as a dodo and completely featherless, so to speak." Sam paused to chuckle at his own joke. "Ain't yer found me yet, mate?"

Saint Peter closed the book with a thud that echoed behind him, on and on into infinity.

"There appears to have been an error," he smiled. "I am afraid you are not expected here until the year 1991, when I believe you expire from -" he coughed, "acute alcoholism."

Sam heaved himself up onto the legs he could no longer see, and faced the old man indignantly.

"Wot d'yer mean, I've got 'ere before me prime? D'yer mean to tell me I was cut down in my prime unnecessarily?" his voice rose onto an even higher querulous tone, "And just before the darts match, too!"

"Oh, it is quite alright," assured the old man hurriedly. "You must go back, dear fellow. You must go back immediately."

"Go back?" gulped Sam in astonishment. "'ere now, 'ang about. 'ew can I go back wivout me perishing body. You've got to let me in now, Guv. Put me name down yourself can't yer?"

Saint Peter sighed.

"My dear man, I could not possibly interfere with Fate. Now, when exactly did you expire? We must get you back before any burial or crematorium arrangements are made."

Sam thought hard.

"It could only have been a few minutes ago. As soon as I realised I had snuffed it, I was looking forward to having a sneaky haunting trip ov me old mates, but lor' luv a duck, I 'ardly 'ad time to close me eyes before some geezer wiv long 'air and noisy flapping wings yanked me out ov me feaver bed and hoisted me on to a soggy cloud. And now 'ere I am, dressed up in me Uncle Albert's old nightgown, by the looks of it."

Saint Peter smiled.

"Still," he insisted, "you must go down and it must be now, Samuel. Already your earthly body is returning to you. You will return before anyone discovers what has happened."

Sam looked down at himself.

"Eh, yer right guv'ner. Look, I've got me fingers back," and he poked them through his invisible body excitedly. However his delighted chortles changed to howls as his fingers found his returning beer paunch rather too enthusiastically.

"Hurry," urged Saint Peter. "Why," he added with a sly smile, "you may even be in time to save your Bible from being buried."

Sam felt the cloud jolt beneath him.

"Goodbye." Sam could hear Saint Peter's voice growing faint. "We'll meet again in 1991. Down you go -"

Down Sam went. He felt giddy.

"Going down, Sir?" he giggled and in a few seconds, the cloud had squeezed itself and cushioned him in through the half open window of his bedroom.

Back in his bed, Sam awoke from what he thought had been a deep sleep. He opened his eyes and then sat up suddenly with a jerk.

"Ellie," he yelled, "Ellie, wat 'ave yer done wiv me blinking Bible?" Sam's eyes opened wider than ever in self-astonishment. "ME BIBLE?" he asked himself, and for the second time that day Samuel Aleysieus Albert Jones had a relapse; temporarily of course!